Eva Marks

little
VALENTINE

EVA MARKS

Copyright © 2023 by Eva Marks

All rights reserved.

No part of this publication may be reproduced, distributed, or transmitted in any form or by any means, including photocopying, recording, or other electronic or mechanical methods, without the prior written permission of the publisher, except as permitted by U.S. copyright law. For permission requests, contact authorevamarks@gmail.com

The story, all names, characters, and incidents portrayed in this production are fictitious. No identification with actual persons (living or deceased), places, buildings, and products is intended or should be inferred.

Book Cover by Eva Marks

A Note from the Author

Little Valentine is a steamy novella, containing explicit and graphic scenes and kinks intended for mature audiences only.

Trigger Warnings
Contains Bondage, BDSM, pet play, sharp objects play and all sorts of edging, a bit of degradation, pregnancy.

.

About the Book

Running a business with Hudson who's my husband, soulmate and Dominant can be as rewarding as it is challenging.

I want to keep pleasing him, be his good girl and the hardworking woman he married and fell in love with.

But when I'm so tired, distracted by my sense of smell that works overtime and uncomfortably bloated, it's hard.

Maybe that's why when Hudson sees through me and demands I take some time off after our Valentine's day tonight, I say yes in a heartbeat.

Because, really, that's all I need. Some rest.

Right?

CHAPTER ONE
Hudson

When all else fails, a cold shower is my go-to.

The season has nothing to do with it, whether it be the crisp cold of the winter months or the warmer summer ones. If my mind needs clearing, then freezing water coursing from the showerhead down my hair and bare muscles do the job. It carries fresh oxygen to my body, invigorating my brain cells, and rerouting dormant paths.

I don't cut corners, and don't spend anything less than ten minutes under the freezing stream.

I don't hide from the pain accompanying it.

I own it, my self-possession is unflappable.

Always have throughout my thirty-seven years on this planet, always will.

It's an innate trait, a force I was born with. And it extends to every aspect of my life.

See, the power I hold over Avery—my beloved submissive twenty-five-year-old wife—the control I have over her and myself alike, it's an extension of me.

It isn't a show. I'm not *acting* a part.

I'm a Dominant with every fiber of my being.

It's been the person I am, even before I educated myself and knew how to label it, manifesting itself first in the non-sexual aspects of my life.

During my school years, I hadn't gone out and partied, hadn't hung around the mall, or spent mindless hours online. I was on a mission: to have a perfect GPA, slay my SATs and nail down my extracurricular activities as a debate team leader, be the head of the swimming team etcetera, etcetera.

I didn't feel like I was missing out. I had a mission: to major in accounting, get a good job, climb the ladder, and get into an MBA program. The sooner the better.

A goal I nailed like a hammer.

Right after my internship at a prestigious accounting firm, I had jobs lined up for me all over the country. I chose to stay on the West Coast, in San Francisco, and started in Whitlock's finance division. Needless to say, I stormed in guns blazing.

I'd spent long hours at the retail company, and studying the business allowed me to come up with improvement suggestions. I'd been confident in my abilities and had no shame whatsoever to present them to higher management, overstepping my bosses, demanding to be heard.

As mentioned, I'm the owner of my reality. While I'm here under the ice-cold water, with one purpose of clearing my head leading me, I'm no different. I'm concentrated, focused, determined.

Just like I have been in the shower today, for the last fifteen minutes or so on this early Wednesday morning in the middle of February. My skin is red, blood rushing through my invigorated body.

Unfortunately, the answers I've come up with are not for the issue I've been seeking to resolve.

For the quarter of an hour I've been here, I've considered and found a solution for the two unresolved issues Avery and I have been facing the past couple of weeks. I've chosen which one of the three suggestions Avery offered to remodel our home office I favored.

Everything's clear as day to me. Clearer than the mirrors decorating our special room for our special taste in sex.

So what in the ever-loving fuck is keeping me from conjuring an idea for a Valentine's gift for my wife?

It shouldn't be this hard. She and I have talked plenty over the three years we worked together. Didn't stop getting to know each other four months later, when we reunited.

Through the eight months of starting a business, getting engaged, and finally getting married two months ago, my wife and I have opened up to each other about any thinkable subject. We talk about everything, all the time.

Part of it is due to our strong bond, the unbreakable love we share.

The other is a result of our lifestyle; if a Dom is oblivious to a crack in the relationship or a sub hiding something from him, for whatever reason, mistakes are bound to follow.

Avery is my one true soulmate, the woman I'd sacrifice my life for if it ever came to that. She's more precious to me than air, the rarest gem created by nature. For me, there's been no one like her, nor will there ever be, and I'll protect, love, and shield her at all costs.

Losing or hurting her would destroy me, both of which we avoid through healthy, constant communication. A concept that can be uncomfortable at times, yet is always necessary. And we stick to it.

But the gift, a truly significant gift, that—I can't think of.

Accepting my temporary failure, I step out of the shower, looking at the vanity in our bathroom to brace for the new day.

I dry off my dark-blond hair, my green eyes staring back at me. There's no question in them. I will find what'll bring Avery genuine joy.

Since it's a no-meeting day, I skip wearing a suit, opting for a long black shirt, a gray cardigan, and blue jeans instead.

Our temporary office is set up in one of the two guest rooms on the top floor. I open the bedroom door to head there and to Avery, who had a head start on the workday.

Silence permeates the hall on my path there, though it's nothing out of the ordinary. Avery rarely talks to her friends on the phone during work hours, her single-minded focus unyielding.

Watching her consumed, passionate about our work sparks a new heat in me every day anew. It reminds me of our days at Whitlock, while we were still nothing but coworkers. How I studied her sitting across from me at my office during our meetings, or how I stole glances at her cubicle when passing by her in the open space of the marketing department.

It's also a symbol of her dedication to the business we're building. This project is a promise of a better work-life relationship for us, for our family. We get to see each other throughout the day, and someday, we'll have the privilege of spending time with our future children; welcome them home from school, and solve math problems together.

Love them.

Our business is slowly taking off, making these dreams a reality one day at a time.

And none of it would've been possible without my wife.

"Little blue," I call her before I make it to the door. "Sorry I'm late, I—"

The rest of my explanation dries up on my lips.

Avery's whitewashed desk faces the expansive windows. The warm February sun filters in to illuminate her station, its bright rays spreading across my wife's long, brown locks. On any other day, the sunlight would have landed on Avery's beautiful face, would have reflected on her wide blue eyes.

They would've sparkled, those eyes I fall more in love with every day, from the moment she opens them until they close in sleep.

On any other day.

At eight-thirty in the morning, my diligent, energetic, and workaholic partner is fast asleep. She has her chin propped on her palm like she couldn't hold herself a second longer. Long eyelashes rest on her soft cheeks, her breaths are slow and quiet.

The lace and leather collar stretches on her neck from this angle, but she doesn't seem to mind it in her severe exhaustion.

My heart twists in my chest, my guilt slapping me across the face.

I've been contemplating long and hard about a gift for her, thinking that another material present, other than the new toy I bought would make this Valentine's perfect for her.

A mistake on my part. I should've realized what's been staring me in the face—above any other toy, jewel, or new dress, Avery needs a rest. A reprieve from the constant *How did the negotiation with the suppliers go?* and *We can allocate more of our resources toward marketing this month.*

We eat, drink, and dream of our company, Cotton for All. Any business would, considering we're in the first stages of opening our ours.

Except we aren't just business partners. Avery is my wife, my sub, my responsibility. Allowing her to slip, to reach this level of exhaustion by missing the signs is a blatant oversight on my part.

I plan on rectifying it. This evening, tomorrow, until the day we retire.

The more her innocent face comes into view as I close the distance between us, the desire to pull her into my arms and protect her intensifies.

My bare feet tread on the hardwood floor until I'm at her side. I look down at her, at the curves, her cobalt-blue shift dress accentuates, at her gentle, innocent features.

It dawns on me that I don't want the workday to start. I'm hungry for my wife's touch, to have this break in our routine for her and myself alike.

To do something that's explicitly *us*.

While caressing the top of her head, I cup the back of her neck to protect her. She seems to be in such a deep sleep, she might be startled and lose her balance if I don't.

"Little blue," I repeat her name, my authority reflecting in the change in my tone.

The louder call and my touch awaken her. I'm right there to catch her when she stirs, my eyes lock on her, injecting clarity into her confusion.

The entirety of me talks to her without uttering a word, stating *I'm here for you.*

Only it doesn't soothe her, not completely.

"Oh my God." Her gaze flicks toward the photo editing program on her computer screen and back to me. "I fell asleep. I can't believe I fell asleep."

"That's okay." My voice settles her with care into the present moment.

"No I—I'm mortified, Hudson." Her cheeks assume a ruddy hue, the change in complexion reaffirming her fluster. "It's so unprofessional, and I— it won't happen again."

"I'm not mad," I'm quick to clarify.

She shouldn't feel this way. The fact that she hasn't collapsed long mornings ago is a borderline miracle. If anyone should be apologizing, it's me, and I'll do it later tonight.

"*I* am." Sleep drifts away from her eyes, the blue in them sharpening. "I have the banners to edit—"

"Not now."

"No?"

"No."

And we start our games.

I trail my hand down to the roots of her hair, tugging lightly.

She squints at me. Not in confusion, nothing like that. Her scent carries to me, the musky fragrance of her swift arousal.

My wife is turned on, but she doesn't lose the battle of her commitment to her work. "It's due for the website later today, for Valentine's, and I haven't finished it."

"Little blue."

"Hudson."

Something in the taunting voice she uses to say my name tells me that suddenly the banner and the deadline aren't as important to her as she lets on.

"It can wait for an hour."

I tug on her hair hard, forcing her eyes to the ceiling and her elegant neck to crane up. I lower my head to hers, so close our breaths mix. I'm the only thing visible to her, and in return, her blue eyes take over my existence.

So perfect.

So submissive.

My wife.

"This morning, this minute, you're mine," I growl. "You'll obey me until I decide it's time to go back to work. Are we clear?"

I pull on her thick locks again for emphasis.

She lets out a heavy breath that ends in a shaky moan. Her smirk doesn't lag to arrive.

"Yes, Sir."

CHAPTER TWO

Avery

Running your own business is absolutely not for the faint of heart.

But having my husband as my partner helps, for sure. Hudson's knowledge and support are true game-changers. There's no question I wouldn't have survived the first week of this without him by my side; his instructions, guidance, trust.

He's my hero.

A hero who works so goddamn hard. He's glued to his desk, adamant about treating me as an equal and teaching me everything he knows. He sleeps less than four hours a night, sneaking out of bed to the office when he thinks I'm sleeping.

And technically, I am, if not for one of the loose floorboards by his side of the bed. It creaks a little. Not enough to lead him to think it could wake me.

It wouldn't have either at any other time when we weren't building a company from scratch.

Adrenaline courses lazily through my veins long after we've gone to bed, resulting in my constant half-asleep half-awake state. The lightest of noises infiltrate my dreams, and maybe that's what finally got to me.

What had me—unprofessionally so—allowing my eyelids to take the wheel and close down shop. I should consider adding herbal tea to my bedtime routine, not just after Hudson fucks me into oblivion.

Speaking of which…

Much like old times, my husband, straightens himself, standing before me fully erect. His cock stands proud in his jeans, his green eyes darken despite the light pouring from the windows.

I'm wet and wanting and am hooked to him and the promise he'll either spank me raw, push my head to the table, or tell me I'm his good girl while his cum drips down my chin.

But it's not the promise of sex stirring a current of electricity beneath my skin. Neither is his beautiful member, whose veins, curves, and power I know by heart and take daily.

Hudson's dominance, that's what does it for me. Even with remnants of sleep clinging to me, the change in his tone, his all-consuming presence, his assertion and control of me—his love language—it's everything to me.

This is Hudson's way of silently telling me *I see you struggling, and you're not alone.*

And by the resolute look his face has taken on, I can tell he won't be soft and sweet while making his point across.

"We're going to role-play. I'm your boss, and as such, I'll be changing into something more appropriate." He speaks, all stern and authoritative. "You'll wait for me here, regardless of how long it takes."

I nod, intent on defeating my exhaustion and agreeing to the fun that doesn't come without the torture of expecting him. Whether it be a minute or an hour, it doesn't matter. It's a sweet kind of pain, equivalent to spanking, and just as delicious.

Because it's through this devotion to Sir that I become invincible. I can conquer any work project. I'm capable of orchestrating any meeting. I experience mind-blowing orgasms.

Simply by obeying.

"Sir?" I ask, remaining seated, beneath him.

He turns his head, glancing at me over his shoulder. "Yes?"

"How do you wish me to wait for you?"

The smirk reaches his eyes faster than it appears on his lips. "In the middle of the room. On your hands and knees."

Another question forms in my gaze.

Hudson, the man who sees into my darkest crevices, answers without me needing to verbalize it. "Leave your clothes on."

"Yes, Sir."

He swivels back to face the door, and in long, self-assured strides, he's out to the hallway.

Rising on my bare feet, I unfold myself from the chair. I heed Hudson's command, lowering my knees, then palms to the floor, ignoring the mild dizziness that ensues.

I really should increase my intake of water, I think.

Then I focus on where I am and what I'm doing. Waiting for him. About to crawl to him. Find atonement for failing to be a professional and staying up on a workday. Hudson said he was not mad, but being here, like this, I realize I am.

Staring at the open door unearths my deep desire to be enough for Hudson.

By doing this, by staying on all fours, I'll show him the devotion I failed to demonstrate at my desk. I'll ignore the stiffness of the floor against my bare knees, I'll accept the cold seeping beneath it and curling around my palms and wrists.

I stretch my ear out, tuning in to Hudson's feet treading across our bedroom. To my Master. Confidence and newfound strength cradle my blood. I am capable. I will satisfy him.

This day will be carved into my consciousness. This waiting, this eagerness to be the best and only partner in this life—in work, beneath the sheets, on my knees, while expecting him as minutes trudge by.

The notion itself sparks a light in my lower belly. The heat grows in the form of branches, twigs, and leaves throughout my body. They lash out to graze my ribs, to engulf my lungs. Their blooms trail higher, finding a home in my breasts.

My arousal for Hudson swallows me whole.

Our office's clock ticks on the wall to my right. An added sign to remind me of the time I've spent in this position. Further fuel to the churning fire in my groin. Every second that passes in this submissive position eats away at my self-recrimination.

I can't wait to have Hudson back. To thank him. To keep doing as he says.

My tongue dries in need while a pool of desire gathers between my legs. My thighs itch to squeeze together, to relieve a part of the mounting pressure. I hold even more still at the thought.

Hudson owns, among other things, my orgasms.

And so, I wait.

The steps on the other side of the hall cease. Curiosity and the fire beneath my skin have me drawing my attention to where he is, picturing him.

Did he buy a new toy to introduce to our sex games? Is he contemplating what to do with me once he's back?

He must be standing there in front of the window overlooking our backyard, being turned on by my expectation of his return. His cock is still rock hard in his jeans, his finger and thumb pinching his stubbled chin or his palm could palm his throbbing erection.

I'm staring at the doorway, my thoughts consuming me as to what my Master might be doing on the other end.

In fact, it enraptures me so much that I don't hear his footsteps when they pick up again, don't realize he's on the move until his frame appears in the hall.

My tongue swipes at my bottom lip, the desire for him almost explosive. If my husband looked striking in his casual jeans, T-shirt, and cardigan, now he appears nothing short of edible in the suit he chose.

Each item he dons on his sculpted body is identical to those he wore the first time he showed up at my apartment. When he was the CFO I lusted over and I was the ex-marketing chick who believed he'd forgotten about her.

Black suit, smoky-gray tie, and shiny black shoes.

"Little one." His voice is thick, lust coating it like a spider's web.

My eyes aren't supposed to be staring at the door, or up. While playing a game, where I'm fully submitted to him, my gaze is to remain on the floor until instructed otherwise.

And that's where I send them at his reproach.

"I'm sorry, Sir."

I should feel more apologetic, but I don't. This little mishap is just another opportunity for Hudson to *fix* me.

His shoes clank on the floor—as steady as the whip his hand turns into when he spanks me. They alert me of his approach. Their tips slide on the floor beneath me next.

The fragrance of his cologne wafts to me. Also the same one from our first non-work encounter eight short months ago.

"It's the second time you apologized today, blue."

My husband's large palm emanates warmth on its travel from the top of my head, all the way down to my chin. He tips it up, signaling me to look at him.

"I appreciate your submission, I really do."

A million stinging bees buzz inside my chest, bringing it to life. His praise does that to me. The simplest word, the most innocuous gesture, they lift me to the heavens.

"However,"—his glare, reproachful and tender, takes ownership of mine—"I won't accept an apology where it isn't warranted."

Wrinkles form on my forehead. We were very clear about the rules, and if we abandon them, if we abandon the structure so freely, it's as if the ground would shake beneath me.

I'm about to ask for clarification, parting my lips, readying my speech.

Hudson's finger on my chin presses it up fast, slamming my lips shut. "I didn't say both apologies were unwarranted. The second one, that's the one I'll make you work for."

CHAPTER THREE
Hudson

"First things first, your eyes."

"Yes, Sir." Avery bites the corner of her mouth, her eyes meeting the floor.

Just like I instructed.

I take a step back.

The action goes against my underlying desire. My self-restraint surges against the deeply-seated need to whip my cock out and have her suck on it, gag on it, have her spit messing up my shoes.

But I do it anyway. Not to punish her, not really.

It's all a part of the game, of the scenario I conjured in my head while making her wait.

"Good girl."

Knowing every piece of furniture, every corner, and every inch of the room, I recognize where my chair is supposed to be. I lower to my seat, crossing an ankle on top of my knee. Pretending to be in full-on work mode.

"Pet,"—I start, not missing out on the whimper she tries to suppress—"come here."

Her hands and knees scrape the floor on their path toward me. She reaches where I sit, stilling at my side. She raises her chin, her gaze remains glued to the wooden floor.

I offer her nonverbal praise, patting her soft hair. My cock swells at the hum it evokes from her, at the delicate flutter of her eyelashes.

"I want to tell you a story." I place both hands on the chair arms, releasing my foot to the floor and spreading my knees suggestively.

"Except I have a problem, you see." My insinuation plus my hand shifting to my hard-on are the subtle hints it requires to have Avery glance in that direction. "These pants, they're fucking suffocating me. I can't think clearly, much less talk with them on."

Ever so slowly, Avery's blue stare climbs to meet my green one. The innocence in it, the question of *How to proceed?* boils my blood a thousand degrees hotter. Despite all the dirty and downright obscene sexual acts we've done, she's managed to cling to that part of her personality.

The Dom in me couldn't have asked for more. To have his sub delve deeper into her hidden desires, her perception of them, and how they can serve me, without losing her true self in the process.

I tilt an eyebrow, faking boredom as another part of my dominance. It serves to remind her duty to work hard for my satisfaction.

Truth is, Avery isn't, nor will she ever be boring.

"You seem confused."

She covers her lips, fingers facing up. Our signal for *May I speak?* while in pet play. I jerk my chin, giving her my approval.

"Do you want me to relieve you, Sir?"

This fucking woman and her deliciously coarse voice.

"Yes, little. That's exactly what I implied."

She resumes her silence, crawling to kneel before me. Her hands glide gingerly to my belt, unbuckling it and getting to work on the button and zipper.

"That's it." Allowing her to get closer, I lean an inch further into the chair. "Much better already."

Avery slips her cheek along my leg, her form of thanking me.

"My praise doesn't mean you did well enough to stop." I wrap my hands around her cheeks, demanding her attention off the comfort of my thigh and to my face. "I asked you to free my dick, and you know how I hate waiting."

Her gasp, that little burst of vocal arousal, is there and gone. What follows is her slender fingers reaching for the waistband of my black boxer briefs.

"So, what I've wanted to tell you, blue." My hunger for Avery is a monster taking shape under my skin. Watching the need mirrored in her ardent focus on my dick and the way her hands work turns it into an insatiable desire. "Is that this is one of the many, many fantasies I've had about you while we worked at Whitlock."

One of my hands returns to the arm of the chair, the other slithers into Avery's lush hair. She uses my favorite conditioner on a daily basis, making each strand smooth in my grip.

She edges her head forward to my bare cock, heavy and fully erect as it rests on my stomach. My grasp on the hair at the base of her scalp tightens like a vise, yanking her back.

"Na-ah. You only take what I give you." The lowering of her gaze sets me on fucking fire, my erection becoming painful. But she won't touch it. Not now.

"There were many, many fucking days where I swear, you'd dress a certain way just to seduce me." I fist myself, tugging on it twice. "Wearing heels an extra inch or two higher, tight skirts to outline the ghost of your garters, even though you wore long blazers pretending to hide them. An open button on your shirt during our meeting that I'd see closed later when we'd meet at the break room."

This is one of the rare topics I haven't asked her yet, and the brief pull of her lips tells me I'm right on the money.

"Greedy little whore." I fasten my hold, forcing her head to tilt upward. A moan of pleasure and pain escapes her, and a drop of precum wets the throbbing head of my cock.

"Look at what you're doing to me." I move her around until she's at eye level with it. "This was the mess you'd make of me those days, in my fucking office. I'd sit with the CEO with precum smearing my boxer briefs because of you."

Her breaths are heavy now, lips parted, a glint of her pink tongue peeking out. I can't fucking take it anymore.

"Lick it." I shove Avery forward, pressing her mouth to my length. "Be a good fucking girl and lick it, just the tip."

A feral growl rips through my lungs when her tongue laps the pearly drop, growing louder when her lips close on it and suck the head.

Applying the minimal ounce of self-control I have left in myself, I wretch her head back. "I said *lick*."

The submissive eyes that stared at me a moment ago have rebellion seeping through them. The light summer blue morphs into a stormy night, the glimmer of her excitement is the lightning slashing into the darkened skies.

"Another reason to punish you." I reach for the desk at my side, still grabbing Avery firmly. "Same as I wanted to punish you back then, for making me feel like I'm losing my mind over you."

My fingers curl around the scissors I've been searching for. "I always thought you were this innocent girl. Even when you fucked with my head. I was unable to picture my unfathomable lust for you reciprocated."

The scissors' blades glint under the glow of the sun, flashing for Avery to see.

"Every meeting you showed up, this unreachable temptress, I was more eager to have you," I say. "Every fucking time, blue."

She doesn't speak, but her hand does the talking for her. It slips to my ankle, massaging the joint under my sock. The simple gesture eats at my tethered state, though none of it will be visible to her.

"That unrequited, insane lust,"—I continue moving forward, leveling my face with Avery's while snapping the scissors open—"it awoke some really, really bad, fucked-up ideas in me. The punishing kind."

I take Avery's mouth the instant I close the scissors' blades on the collar of her dress.

Snip.

The fabric tears easily. I suck on Avery's tongue to muffle her surprised cry. I snap them open and cut the rest of the dress to the center front of her bra, then pull away.

"I wanted you to hurt for what you did to me."

After releasing her head, I shove the sleeves of her dress, exposing her black bra to me.

"Wanted to punish you, so your pussy would soak through your panties and your ass would be red from my palm." I lick across my upper teeth, calculating what to do next. "Straighten up on your knees. Now."

She does, sitting there with her torn dress. Her tiny nipples poke through the lace bra, hot and begging for me to devour them in my mouth.

I yank down the cups of her bra, freeing her plush mounds to hang over the wires. I do a double take, wondering if I'm imagining things or if they've gotten bigger.

A quick math in my head tells me her time of the month is close. It can't be a pregnancy. She stopped taking the pills once we tied the knot, but it's not like we've been actively trying. And it's only been two months.

Can't be.

Not that I would object to it. Hell, a child with my wife is the equivalent of hitting life's jackpot or drawing the lottery's winning numbers. The best there is.

But she would've told me if she was late. I'd rather not get my hopes up.

The remaining option is PMS.

And while some might complain about the added hormones, I have not one bad word to say about my wife. I love her mood swings—they're hers, and therefore, mine—and am aroused by them all.

The swelling breasts are just a bonus.

"You're no longer my pet, little." Her left tit is soft to my cruel pinch of her flesh. "You may talk."

"Do it, please," she rushes to say, her voice hoarse and seductive. "Punish me. Make me regret it, make me be a good girl for you, Sir."

CHAPTER FOUR

Avery

Hudson doesn't hesitate, pinching my nipples with both hands.

To the echo of my grunt, he twists and draws them toward him. They stretch and erect under his tweaks and it hurts so good, tears well behind my eyes. Any other nipple torture he inflicted in the past is nothing compared to this one rousing inside me.

I want more. More punishment, more pain, more mind-eclipsing pleasure.

And Hudson knows me well enough not to give me any of it.

His name slips out of my lips as a throaty cry when he switches from hurting me to rubbing the tender flesh between his fingers.

"Punishment, little." He opens his palms, allowing my yearning mounds the slightest of touches by rolling the inside of his palms up and down, grazing them ever so tenderly. "Remember?"

The only thing keeping my scream bottled up is my teeth's stronghold on my lower lip. This barely-there caress sends me into a spin. I'm hurting all over, craving my Sir in a way that's out of control.

He finally leaves my breasts alone, returning to hold the scissors. Hudson snip, snip, snips them at my dress, straight down the middle, reaching my panties, and then he puts them away.

"Mmm." He bends forward, his hot hum spreads goosebumps on my skin faster than I'm able to fathom what he does to me. "So wet."

Hudson's fingers shove ruthlessly beneath my panties and into my slit, curling inside His rough thrusts and my juices produce inelegant slurping sounds, and my husband grins against my skin.

"You made a mess of your panties, Avery." He closes his lips on my shoulder, sucking hard. My hips buckle, straining for his touch. "Such a sopping mess. I believe they're no longer usable."

The most obscene words in the English language always have a way of sounding deliciously classy when they're spoken from his mouth.

"Yes, Sir." I nod, my cheek rubbing the short hair of his head. "I really ruined them, haven't I?"

His teeth pierce my skin. I do everything in my power not to yelp. To be his behaving submissive.

Then I'm bereft of his mouth and his fingers. In their stead arrive the scissors. They slide along my pussy, clipping away at my panties. The tip reaches my hood, parting my folds as Hudson sways it left and right.

"Easy there," Hudson, once again reading my mind, warns me against flinching. "I won't harm you. Not ever. I just…"

His words trail the farther south the scissors go. He doesn't pin them to my clit, doesn't risk the sharp edge harming me. He just…

"Want to play," he finishes his sentence, completing my trail of thought.

To say I'm soaking wet would be to belittle and disregard the experience I'm partaking in. My mouth is dry, my heart is pounding to the point of pain. My blood rushes and clanks behind my ears, a massive train running on shaky rails.

Boom, click, boom.

"Hudson." I throw a hand desperately at his knee.

The immense pleasure this fear brings is weakening, stealing my ability to hold steady.

"Blue."

My panties fall to either side of my hips after the last cut has been done. But he doesn't remove the blade.

"This… This is what I had in mind for you." He cups my jaw, his other hand still tormenting my clit. Left, right, left the blade goes. "To tear off the clothes you knew would get under my skin, have you naked and at my mercy."

"I—I—" I start. The whirlwind at the bottom of my navel prevents any coherent sentence from emerging.

The floor beneath my knees doesn't bother me. The tethered dress is nothing except two ripped pieces of fabric.

But Hudson's minty breath, his fiery eyes, his unrelenting pursuit to unravel me with these scissors slipping across my wetness—that takes me apart piece by piece. It leaves me truly naked, wholly Hudson's.

"I wanted you blubbering, on your knees, not a piece of clothing on that hot little body." He presses our foreheads together. "Wanted you mine."

My breasts are weighed down by my lust, my existence twisting and turning into a bomb ready to explode.

"Please."

"Please, what?" He dips the dull blade of the scissors to the top of my slit, making it wet and dragging them up to my clit, resuming his teasing. It doesn't hurt, and I trust Hudson so fully that I give in and revel in it.

"Please, Sir." The words are vowels and consonants, things my brain remembers, though at the present moment mean absolutely nothing to me.

"What would my greedy employee have asked for?" His hand slithers to my breast, forcing me to grab his knee tighter to balance myself. "If we were to do it back then?"

"Let me come," I rasp.

"What about *Sorry for being a cock tease, Sir*?"

This isn't a rhetorical question, my lost mind manages to comprehend it. He commands me to say it.

He presses a button in me, and I do it. There really is no other option when my impending orgasm depends on it; when I'm aware that another one of these sentences might drive me over the edge.

I lower my chin, looking at Hudson beneath my eyelashes. "I'm sorry for being a cock tease, Sir."

"Christ." He loses the scissors.

One minute I'm on my knees, the other I'm in the air, and then on my back. He kicks my legs to each side, baring my hot, pulsating pussy to him.

"The way you said it, fuck." He removes his suit jacket, towering over me. "This orgasm is mine to feel on my cock, to squeeze and milk it. Not around air. On. Me."

"Yes, Sir."

My body breaks out in tremors, understanding exactly what he's talking about. The buildup is winning me over, and when it comes, it'll wreck me.

"Arms over your head, little," he grates out.

He demands, and I follow.

"After you would've begged me so nicely,"—his teeth scrape my cheek—"asked for my forgiveness like the good girl you are, I would've bound your wrists."

The blunt crown of his cock grazes my hypersensitive clit and my navel on his journey up my body. He's at my raised hands, lifting them off the floor to tie his coat around my wrists as he described. Like he'd done on our first sexual encounter.

"I wouldn't take my shirt off, wouldn't have given you that." His lips tilt in a sly smirk. "The furthest your apologies would've gotten you was to have my cock in your tight little cunt. Fuck you nice and hard."

The word *please* must leave my mouth a million times, I'm so desperate for him.

And my husband satisfies the burning ache with one swift thrust.

"Fuck," I cry out, my insides as ripped as my clothes.

As wet as I am, as many times as Hudson fucked me in the past, his size is something I'll never get used to. The thick, demanding cock pounds at me one thrust after the other.

His strong palm brackets my face from one side; his other one slips between us, twisting my clit, challenging my will, daring me to defy him.

I will not.

"Hudson," my breath is being knocked out of me as he delivers merciless pummeling into my cunt.

"Almost," he grunts out, then lowers his lips to steal mine.

He ravages me with his mouth, invades me with his tongue and I'm flying high above the ground. I'm in the clouds, held by Hudson, loved by the universe.

Nothing will ever bother me again.

"Now," he says between lips and bites. "Come for me, little one. Make me yours."

And I do. In a white-hot flash of light, my body releases what it's been working diligently to hold on to. The eruption rattles my bones, my pussy clenching and unclenching to the pace of my moans.

"That's a good girl," Hudson growls, fucking me to the floor. "Fuck. That's a very fucking good girl."

He grips the area beneath my knee, pinning it to my chest. Grace and elegance are embodied in his brutal thrusts, love, and devotion in his violent kisses.

"Come again, baby," he demands. Sweat coats his forehead, the scent mixing with that of his cologne. "Give me another one."

It feels like it'll hurt. It feels like it'll scorch my insides.

It feels, above all, like it'd satisfy my Sir. I get over the bullshit in my head, throw away the fear, and allow myself this scary, miraculous free fall.

The second wave of pleasure thunders inside me. I'm open and closed, freed and chained all at once.

"Fuck, yes," he lets out one last time, before releasing his sperm in a few brutal thrusts.

Our erratic breaths slow within minutes of descending from this experience. During those countless seconds, Hudson's fierce glare reverts to the imposing, yet sweet Dom he is.

His punishing hands are now couriers of affection. Leaning on his forearms, he strokes one of my temples while kissing the other, ensuring his body warmth protects me as my own drops.

"You did so well," I hear him say from above me as he undoes the tie.

"Thank you, Sir." Though the scene technically ended, I would never think of Hudson as anything but my Sir. Nothing is taken from me when I say that, but much is given.

"I love you, blue," he murmurs to my skin on our way to our bedroom. I'm cradled in his arms, my head buried in his chest. "I love you so goddamn much."

"I love you, too." My nose finds its home in Hudson's shirt, sniffing the smell of *him*. "I really do."

CHAPTER FIVE

Avery

I'm tired. It makes a hell of a ton more sense at the moment, compared to earlier.

Hudson took and manipulated my body and mind to both our pleasure. Our game carried me to the verge of losing my mind and self in him. The rediscovery of myself and my adoration for my husband thrusts me to the highest of highs as well as taking its toll on me.

Fortunately, Hudson, the master of my heart, is also a master in aftercare. And that he does.

"Little one," he coos.

Even his sweet talk has dominance laced into it, and it comforts me. I don't want to be anywhere else other than under his all-powerful, nurturing dome.

I stare back at him, then around me in our bedroom. At our home.

Since I moved in, I haven't changed much other than the office. Hudson designed his Mediterranean

Revival home with as much class as he applies to the rest of his life.

Besides, there are memories of us in each corner, in every blue and gold, and on the king-size bed I'm currently lying on top of.

The white-wash nightstands had been there on my sleepovers during our engagement period, the antique-styled night lamps standing on them have shed a soft glow on my skin while Hudson draped kisses on it over and over before I droned to sleep on many, many nights.

He's bought the bright blue throw pillows to stand out in the middle of the cream-colored sheets and pillows because he said that way, he could always have a piece of me with him.

It would pain me deeply to dispose of a single item or have new ones that will only serve to intrude on the current state of things.

"I'm here." I blink away the drowsiness weighing heavy on my eyes.

"I know. Have this." Hudson tucks my hair behind my ear, holding a chocolate bar to my lips. "You seemed a bit floaty. How are you feeling?"

My attention flickers to his bare chest, to the light smattering of hair. He eventually did take his shirt off, heeding my request after he was finished. Whatever I ask of my husband outside of a scene, and especially during the aftercare moments, he does it in a heartbeat.

Today, in particular, I wanted to cuddle into his warm skin, to mold into his flesh.

"I'm good." I nibble on the chocolate. The funny taste causes me to make a face. "What's the expiration date on this one?"

In his worry, Hudson's eyebrows knead together as he examines the wrapping.

"Expires in three months." Some of the tension simmers off his somber expression. "But it goes to the trash now."

"That's so weird." Chocolate forgotten, I snuggle into the crook of Hudson's neck.

"What would you like to have instead?"

His hand threads through my hair, applying the slightest pressure to beckon me to him. Though Hudson navigates most of the attention of the aftercare on me, he needs my affection to return him to safety, too. Less than I do, but when he seeks out my closeness, I'd rather die before I refuse it.

"You."

He chuckles. "You have me."

I melt.

A couple of minutes are coated in silence.

"What else, really?" he insists. "I can run you a bath. Order an early lunch. Sing you to sleep."

At the last word, the lethargy surrounding me evaporates. "No!"

"No to what?"

"No to sleep." I try to wrangle myself out of his embrace and fail. His arms lock me to him, his chin resting at the top of my head, affectionate, though not an inch less possessive. "Sleep? Really? It's not even ten in the morning. I have so much work to get done."

"Well, love, it feels like you might need it." His fingers mark my skin beneath the T-shirt of his I'm wearing. "For one, you fell asleep on your desk."

Shame fills me. It's then that I'm a tiny bit glad he hasn't let me move, free from having to look at him past my embarrassment. "Which I apologized for."

"Which I said you have no reason to apologize for." The smoothness of his touch as he skims his hand along my torso and up to my neck reinforces his point. "It's my fault. I should've picked up on it earlier. Should've called for a second break throughout the day. Or something."

Nine times out of ten, I don't scold Hudson for caring for me when he addresses me as his sub and his wife.

But when it's our business, however, it's a different story. We're partners, no one beneath the other. He himself proved it time and again, his respect and how he views me as an equal.

So, this, this taking the blame on himself or demanding breaks without consulting me irritates me.

I suck in a long, relaxing breath, reminding myself of his good intentions, that his reactions are love-fueled and not arrogant.

"Hudson."

"At the very least, not let it seep into the night." He's too lost in his remorse to listen to me, I sense it in his faraway tone. "There has to be a divider between office life us and the real world us. Has to be."

I kiss his collarbone gently, opening my mouth to nibble on his neck.

"You're trying to distract me." The smile I hear in his voice tells me he's returned to me.

"Is it working?"

"Indeed." He pulls back, holding me by the shoulders. "Avery."

"Hudson."

"We have ground rules for our sexual and emotional relationship." His head tilts. "Setting ones for our business partnership shouldn't be any different."

"But…" I consider his logic, then consider how to communicate my opposition to it. "Sleeping can't be a part of it."

"I don't mean naps on a regular basis. You're not cut out for it and neither am I. I'm talking about what led to your spontaneous crashing, and how we make sure we won't end up there again."

"When you say it like that." I let the tension slide off my shoulders and my resistance slips from my heart.

Hudson isn't in the habit of making selfish decisions or imposing rules on me because of the nature of our dynamic. And I do feel as if my body is forcing me into the sleep I refuse to give him, now and earlier today.

"What do you suggest?"

"We stop working the minute we"—he does air quotes—"*leave* the office. We decide on an hour, depending on the day, our meetings, deadlines, schedule. It can be five, it can be ten. But it'll be a set time, and it won't be after eight for over three nights a week."

"What about video calls in Europe and Asia?"

He nods. "The rare ones we have, we'll make an exception. Not before we navigate to a time that works both ways."

"Okay." I scour my brain for hardships I stored away in my attempts to not disappoint him and myself. "No work calls, either."

"No work talk, too."

Another crucial aspect flashes before my eyes. And to think I was ready to seal our agreement before nailing that one. "Definitely no sneaking out in the middle of the night."

His eyebrow arches. "You fake sleeping?"

I pin my chin to my chest, giving him a look of *Really?*

"The faker blaming me for faking?"

"Fair enough." Hudson's easy smile ravishes me, dousing me in his sweet, virile heat. "The floorboard gave me away, didn't it?"

"I'll never tell."

His eyes narrow, but this time they glimmer with sweet, uncharacteristic mischief. Then his hands are at my sides, tickling me while his honed body pins me to the bed.

"I surrender!" I yell-giggle. "Yes, it did."

He stops his tickle attack, but his body remains looming over mine. The warmth from the curl of his lips travels lightning-fast right into my heart. One day I'm bound to get lost in my husband's glory, never to be found again.

"Deal?" I break the moment.

"Deal." He kisses my forehead.

With the grave talk behind us, I allow myself the pleasure of teasing him. "Hudson, I've been curious about something."

"Why didn't I fix the floorboard?"

I'm so not accustomed to him being funny that it catches me by surprise. My whole face scrunches for an instant before my brain analyzes what Hudson said and I crack up.

"You're good at this," I point out once I'm settled. "At being funny."

"*You* make me good at it."

He lowers to his forearms, plastering his body to mine. The position and his out-of-character humor—on a workday morning, no less—take away about five years from both him and me alike.

I've had my reservations about Hudson's warm and cuddly side, contrary to the Dominant I fell in love with. But the more time we spend together, the more I've come to realize I don't need Hudson to be a frowning ball of somberness twenty-four-seven. I need him to be himself. I need him to be happy.

I need him to be human in order for me to be those things, as well.

"So, little, what's been bothering this wonderful mind of yours?"

My eyes dance between his, and I suppress the smile bubbling behind my lips. "Does this dominance thing work on me while I sleep?"

The corners of his eyes crinkle. "Do explain."

"Can you, I don't know, slither into my dreams, tell me *No work here, either* and spank me if I do it the following night?"

"Trust me, I would if I could," he laments, and I believe him fully. "What I *can* do though is be your Valentine's date for tonight."

Remembering our Halloween holiday party at a sex club, I can't help but ask, "At Fly High?"

"No." His eyes darken, his memories working similarly to mine. "Tonight, it's you and me.

Candlelit dinner at a nice place where I'll get to wine and dine my wife."

From many other men, this would sound like a cliché. Men who aren't my husband. He isn't asking me out to conform to society. This isn't for him to mark a mandatory item on his spousal to-do list. Whatever my Hudson does, he does it because he means it.

And I say yes to the first Valentine's date in my life.

CHAPTER SIX
Avery

"Dude, how are you?" Jen, my best friend, says at rapid speed, merely letting me finish the word *hello.*

I turn to Hudson who's at his desk, still, in the suit he wore earlier. I asked him to keep it on, and being the man he is, he obliged. Easily.

His lips twist in a smile, meaning he overheard Jen hollering over the phone's speaker without taking a pause from typing away at his laptop.

"I'm uh—okay."

My answer comes out clipped, less friendly than it would've been had she called tonight. I don't make it a habit to answer the phone for personal calls during the day or very late into the evening. It feels wrong, even more so that Hudson and I just finished setting out what work hours are earlier today.

And four o'clock in the afternoon is definitely a part of the workday.

"How, uh"—my head's deep in the online catalog from a supplier we've been negotiating with sent us, refusing to disconnect—"how are you, Jen?"

Hudson's typing silences. His eyes cross to mine, his green gaze is partly sly and mostly sweet. This and his tilted eyebrow are his non-verbal signs telling me it's okay to talk to my friend.

Throughout the months we've been together, he's been very adamant that I don't lose myself too much in work and our relationship that I miss out on my youth and friends. His approval is a given.

I'm the one who needs to be fine with it.

"I'm good, weirdo." She laughs. "I feel like we haven't talked in forever."

My husband gets up slowly. He walks over to me, kisses the top of my head, and mouths *tea?*

The morning's fatigue hasn't waned completely, and I nod and mouth back, *Thank you.*

Inside my chest, my heart does a double flip-flop. Hudson would've never asked me to talk outside the office, I'm aware of it. It doesn't change my appreciation of him. How I don't take an inch of what he gives me for granted.

He leaves silently, and I stare at his broad, delicious back until he disappears.

"Are you there? Avery?"

"Yes, yes." I swallow around the lump of *feelings* clogging my throat. I really wish my period would start already and blow away this emotional bubble. "I am now, can you repeat what you said?"

"Now that we're no longer on a Hudson Pause." She huffs a laugh at the name.

"Har har."

Hudson is a handsome, magnetizing species of man. I told Jen so, numerous times when I blamed my ogling him for being spaced out during our late-night conversations. And so, the Hudson Pause was born.

I spin toward the table, resting my cheek on my forearm. "Glad to provide you entertainment, lady."

"You have. To me and Briar." She sniggers and her boyfriend yells in the background *Liar.*

"You're the liar, not me," she teases him. "By the way, Aves, why are you sounding squished?"

"Sorry." I realize my forearm blocks my coherent speech ability, straightening in the chair overlooking the street. "Slumped on my desk for a second, there."

"You? Slumping? A form of rest? What's wrong?" Her tone turns reproachful. "You never needed rest."

"I never owned a company, either."

I sigh, looking over my shoulder. Hudson isn't back yet, and though I have absolutely no secrets from him, I feel bad having him be an audience to this for a second time today.

"Are you okay?" Jen's love seeps through the phone. "You need a girls' night? Just the two of us?"

"I do, but not because I'm not doing well. I'm really okay. More than okay." My eyes tear up. I blink back the annoying liquid. "I love it. I'm not sure what's come over me. I think a good night's sleep would solve about half my problems."

"Oh." She sounds mildly disappointed.

"Oh? Oh, what?"

"Nothing." Jen hums, her voice trailing. "Nothing at all."

"You know you can't unsay it, right?"

"Ugh, fine. But let the record show I didn't want to say it to let you rest."

"Duly noted."

Hudson's shoes announce his arrival, the scent of the hot coffee follows. I stand up to return the courtesy and leave the room for him to work when his large palm lands on my shoulder.

I glance up at him, encountering my favorite mug in his hand and the subtle shake of his head. He says nothing, placing the mug on my desk and returning to his chair.

"—for a double date tonight."

Despite zoning out again, I manage to decipher the end of my friend's question.

"I'd love to." I walk over to Hudson's desk to give him an inaudible peck on the cheek. I look at him, knowing he'll reply with an *Absolutely* to Jen's proposal. He would.

It's me who wouldn't.

"Over the weekend, maybe?"

"You guys are hanging onto that honeymoon phase, I see."

"Give the poor girl a rest." I hear the echo of Briar's joke.

Hudson's teeth flash in a naughty grin. I roll my eyes, lowering the phone's volume.

"Will not. She's my best friend, she earned this."

"Well, yes, yes we are in the honeymoon stage. All the time." I wink at Hudson who wiggles his finger at me. Then I yawn. "Anyhow, I have to cut this short. So yes, we're going on a Valentine's date, just the two of us tonight, but what about Saturday night? The four of us, music, drinks, dinner?"

"Robel's?" She refers to the bar she and I used to go to every Friday night after work to welcome the weekend.

"Yes, Robel's would be perfect. Eight thirty?" I direct the question to her and Hudson.

He raises a thumb and Jen squeals, "Yes!"

I end the call, about to pick up work where I stopped.

"Little blue."

His name for me draws me to him harder than a leash.

"Yes?"

"I'm up for a double date tonight." He swivels away from the screen, giving me his full attention. "If it makes you happy, we'll do it."

Hudson will shamelessly boss me around on many matters. *Get on your knees, Wear that blue blouse for me today*, and his latest one, *You need to rest more.*

What he hasn't and will never do, is separate me from the outside world. He embodies what I need him to be to a T—loved and protected, and all the while the owner of the keys to my kingdom.

"I know you"—I cover my lips when another yawn escapes—"do. I just want my husband to myself tonight."

"You have me." His smooth forehead wrinkles. "You always have me. Why don't we go out on a different night? Call it our Valentine's?"

"I'm fine, really." The warm coffee makes it easier to gulp down my throat. "Nothing caffeine won't fix."

"Little, you're yawning. A lot." His wrinkles transform into deep creases, his voice a low rumble. "I'm this close to vetoing tonight. I won't let you wear yourself down."

"No." I whip my head left and right. "I swear, I would've communicated if it was something more than a yawn."

"Okay." Hudson's lungs expand like he's going to add a questioning sentence. He snaps them shut, deciding on, "I trust you."

Three simple words, which I have every intention to be worthy of.

CHAPTER SEVEN
Hudson

My wife snuck in a cup of coffee while I was out jogging.

We closed our office at six p.m., leaving enough time for me to go on a half an hour jog around the block and for her to hit the shower.

But she didn't.

I unlock the front door to our home, stepping inside the foyer. To get to the kitchen, I have to go through an arched doorway, past the living room and breakfast room, around twenty-five feet in total.

The scent of the coffee I set up in the early morning shouldn't permeate through that distance. A fresh batch would.

Remaining exactly where I am, dripping sweat in my running gear, I take a moment to consider this.

On one hand, I promised Avery to trust her when she said she's okay, that she's not that tired.

Trust is absolute, and it works both ways. She knows my word is my vow, and I really, really fucking want to believe hers is the same.

I want to believe this early morning snooze and yawns throughout the day aren't a sign of anything graver. I'm keen and desperate to take her word for it, hating how I stand here contemplating the meaning behind this second coffee.

I'm determined to trust her.

Then again, on the flip side, therein lie my responsibilities to her. I ought to look out for her first and foremost.

After all, it's why I suggested dinner. My aim was to engage both of us in something fun, something outside of the work environment. For her and me alike.

Yes, I love eating and drinking with her. I love her flushed face when I tell her I'm so proud of her in public, the anticipation that builds for the both of us.

But the primary reason for this date is Avery. It kind of defeats the purpose if she's wiped out, turning our date into a burden rather than escapism.

"Hudson?"

Fuck. She heard the door.

There isn't much time for me to assess my options. They're pretty clear-cut, the way I see it. One, I can either comment on the coffee and use it as evidence to reschedule our date, or two, I can believe Avery, trust her to tell me the truth, and pretend like nothing's changed since I left for my run thirty minutes ago.

"In here."

The keys clank inside the console the same instant I opt for trusting my wife. She could've wanted coffee for coffee's sake. She likes the taste. There's nothing more to it.

"Good." She speed-walks to me.

My love meets me halfway in the living room, her smile wide and her hand holding a mug. The knot bounding my lungs relieves some more; she's not hiding it. There's no hidden meaning behind it, she's not pretending she hasn't drunk anything by getting rid of the evidence.

It's coffee. Just coffee.

I open my arms and my heart to receive her landing. She thrusts the empty cup onto the coffee table, proceeding to lodge herself into me. Her cheek rests on my sweaty chest, her eager fingers crawl underneath the jacket and beneath my damp shirt, massaging the muscles of my back.

Her nearness and knowing touch get me hard in a heartbeat.

Mirroring her movements, my hands slide under the T-shirt of mine she's wearing, running along the slender curve of her spine.

"I missed you," she mumbles into me.

"Already?" I snap her bra open.

"M-hmm." Avery, in subtle grinds, sways her belly to my length. "Looks like you missed me too."

I groan, tracing her prickly skin with the pads of my fingers all the way to the sides of her breasts. I feel her moan through my jacket, tense when one of her hands deviates from rubbing my back to slipping under my waistband and caressing my hip.

"Dirty girl." I grasp her jaw, angling her to me. "Is that why you haven't showered? Wanted to wait to be covered in your Sir's sweat?"

My fingers dent her butt, pulling her to me. I swallow her gasp in my lips, devouring the air she breathes. Her tender, searching tongue matches her sweet scent.

As always, I take that innocence, twisting and shaping it into something sinister. I dive my tongue behind her teeth, applying more power to the grip I have on her jaw. She moans under the added pressure, the forceful invasion. I draw her even closer.

Avery's lips stop warring against mine, her muscles relaxing. She's pliant, agreeable to anything I might do to her. And I do, sucking and nipping her bottom lip while rolling my tongue on the bottom of it. Never really cruel, and only barely-just kind.

"Yes," she rasps, pulling me to her. "I wanted you. Everything about you."

I run my teeth down her neck, to that sweet spot where her shoulder and throat connect. At this point, even her hands are no longer functioning. She leans her weight into me, giving me permission to continue doing with her as I will.

"Let's see if you really mean it." Slipping my palm to the back of her panties, I trail it along her crack. "Let's see how much of a filthy girl you are."

The front of her body jerks forward as my thumb traces the rim of her asshole. I drag it in slow circles, nudging it inside her.

"Yeah," I hum into her skin, then bite. "To the world, you are my perfect, pristine, wife, but we both know you love being a nasty whore for me, don't you?"

"Yes," she yells, her thighs beneath me.

"Say it." I extend my index finger to her pussy, playing with the dripping juices of her arousal and my cum.

Her warm breath flutters on the short hairs on my neck, her ass clenching and unclenching in her despair to pull me deeper.

"Use your words." Halting everything I do, I remove my hand, letting it hover above her needy holes. "Or I'm sending you to shower alone, little."

She groans, the sound rippling through me. "I'm your dirty whore, Sir. I'm your filthy, desperate slut and I need you to clean me up."

"You take instructions so well." I dip my fingers deep inside her in a blunt strike. "So fucking well."

"Thank you,"—she says, the words being torn out of her mouth—"Sir."

Overwhelmed by my power and desire for her, I don't spare another minute. I bend my knees an inch, align my hands above her panties and hoist Avery in the air. In an urgency parallel to mine, she rummages her hands to my nape, crossing her ankles at my waist and pressing me to her.

Our hunger and mutual desire are in perfect angsty harmony. Hands clawing at clothes, teeth scraping skin, growls and moans materializing in our chests and floating into the air.

But it's too messy. Too unorganized. And I, as well as my wife, crave the structure.

I break our kiss, staring into her eyes. "Go to the bathroom."

Her blue eyes dance, attempting to make sense of my words. I reach behind me to peel her legs from around my waist. It's then that she understands, slowly, and in her rush to do as I say, she descends to the floor.

"I won't repeat myself."

Biting her lower lip, her wild, brown hair flails from one side to the other as she shakes her head. She spins on her heel, climbing the stairs with a sway of her hips.

"Move it, little," I say while cupping my raging erection, sliding my hand over it to take off the edge.

What Jen calls the "honeymoon stage," I deem as the "forever stage." I don't see a scenario where I'll ever tire or be bored of playing with and fucking Avery. Not solely for how impeccably compatible we are, in bed in terms of kinks and what gets us off. Nor is it due to Avery's curves and the way my hands mold to her flesh like she was made for me.

The complete and utter synchronization of our souls, that's what turns me on. There won't be a day, a minute, an hour when I won't want to bury my dick in her, because I will love her until my dying breath.

With these thoughts in my mind and my dick in hand, I watch her go up in the direction of our bedroom. Only after the water starts running in our bathroom do I follow her there.

"Well, well." I step inside our room, perching myself against the doorway, observing her. "What do we have here?"

Avery sits on her knees naked, her collar off as well so the water won't ruin it. Her palms are face up, eyes on the marble floor. I fold my arms over my chest, pleased to find her as eager to play for the second time today as I am.

She controls the explosive energy I witnessed on the ground floor.

I fucking adore her for it.

Though this isn't where my admiration for her ends. In the short minutes she had here by herself, she managed to set the scene to fire up every nerve ending under my skin.

The warm glow of the vanity plays on Avery's soft body, highlighting her beauty. Her song choice, *Love is A Bitch* by Two Feet, filters through the speakers, laying another sensual layer to the already sensual evening we started early.

"I'm ready for you, Sir."

"I can see that." I pace forward, casting my shadow over her. "And I'm so proud of you. For the whole setting. Now, stand up."

One curt nod comes before her yielding.

"Go check on the water," I say, looking down at the top of her head. "I don't want you to get burned."

She gets to it, pulling open the doors to the shower. She restrains her movements to short, deliberate steps, stretching out her hand with equally meticulous precision. She doesn't do anything I haven't ordered, becoming a vessel for my pleasure.

"Back to me."

Equally compliant, she paces in my direction. The hot water's steam curls around the bathroom, warming up the room further. Avery's arousal is evident, her nipples pointing forward. Hard, pink pebbles I can't get enough of sucking, licking, and biting on.

"We're going to get very fucking dirty before we go out today." My fingers wind in her hair, pulling it to have her eyes on me. "You're going to be my whore before you're my lady. But we can't do any of that if we're not clean, can we?"

"No, Sir."

"Good girl." My voice doesn't rise over a whisper. "You have two minutes to take my clothes off."

CHAPTER EIGHT
Avery

Hudson's dominance wreaks havoc on my sanity. The exhaustion that's returned about an hour after the four p.m. coffee is once more swiped under the rug. Nonexistent, nondisruptive.

Life's troubles and minor inconveniences accumulate to nothing when he exerts his control over me.

When he loves me in his special way.

He pinches my clit while I'm lost in his eyes.

I scream.

Hudson adds a twist to the existing pain. "Who's the one doing the waiting in our relationship, little?"

"I am." The surprising, sharp sting causes my statement to sound like a question.

"You're not sure?"

He beckons me to the wall, my bundle of aching nerves between his fingers. Aching and delighted, because fuck, only he can do it so it hurts so good.

And the pleasure amps up higher when he releases me all at once. Blood floods to my clit, and the quick rush of feelings amplify the sensations as if it's Hudson's lips there, lapping his tongue, kissing me ardently.

"Hudson," I moan, throwing my hands to the wall.

"No." He paces back. Two steps that become an erected wall in the middle of the bathroom.

"Please."

"That's an improvement."

His somber expression doesn't waver. He doesn't grimace at my intense need for him. His composure serves to remind me I am there to please him, and I'm failing.

My eyes well up.

What the fuck is this? I know it's a game. I know I don't *actually* disappoint him.

I bite the inside of my cheek until I almost draw blood. Anything to pull back the tears.

Hudson's head tilts a little. "Your safeword. Give it to me, now."

"Whitlock." I force a smile, telling him the only truth available to me through this mess of emotions. "I just want to be good."

"You are." He masters the change in his tone, shifting it slightly to communicate he's not upset. "You're my good little girl. Always were, always will be."

"I'm the one waiting." I heave out a long breath, assuming my part. "Not you, never you."

"Come here." His arms spread to the side, welcoming me.

My feet lead me to him, to do as he asked. No coddling nor a second request is needed for me to start working on his jacket.

His zipper rolls down, baring his damp shirt. It clings to his body, outlining his abs, accentuating the sculpted ridges of his chest. I push the insides of his sleeves, relieving him of his jacket.

"Avery."

"Let me do this."

The desperation to feel *normal* stops me from questioning this unexplained change in me. I tug on the hem of his shirt, the sleek fabric of his thermal rolling between my fingers.

He doesn't budge.

"I need to do it." I meet his gaze, willful and determined to go through with it. "Sir."

He nods. The toned muscles of the front of his body tense and release beneath my fingers as he raises his arms. The shirt slips off, messing his hair up a tiny bit. Hudson's scent of sweat and male infiltrates my nose, the closeness of his naked body usurps my view of anything else.

Trailing my hungry eyes up, the air whooshes out of my lungs with my husband's intensity.

Whether he attempts to read me or devour me alive, I have no way of telling.

All I know is that I have to keep moving, have to march forward in this act of service. I'm loved and belong harder than ever, and this is what I do to maintain this feeling of normalcy.

I kneel to the floor, untying Hudson's shoelaces. He grasps the back of my scalp when I remove each one, dragging me to him in the process. More of his virile scent, of his beautiful cock fills me and I sigh with desire while removing Hudson's socks, one after the other.

"You're doing so well," he praises me, his hoarse voice adding sensuality to the air around us. He strokes my hair as I straighten on my knees. "Take off my pants. I know my dirty girl wants my cock and I'm so fucking ready for you."

Relief washes over me, hearing the hint of command in his voice.

My calling.

My fingers hook into Hudson's waistband, shoving it and his boxers to his feet. His thick dick juts out, heavy and veiny and absolutely mine.

A dark desire permeates through me in the process of undressing him. I pull off Hudson's sweats and boxers to the side, away from his feet, but I don't stand up immediately.

Instead, I bend even lower to a bowing position. Saliva rushes to my mouth, an acute pang of heat pooling at my pussy. And then I lick his big toe.

"Fuck," he groans, my ravenous need for him reflected in his voice.

I repeat the motion, this time opening my lips to suck on it. He curses again. I continue to his other toes, ascending to the surface of his foot, inhaling in and licking his ankle.

Hudson's body gives off a low vibration. I slant my head upward, getting more motivated, more aroused by my husband jerking himself. His hand squeezes and strokes, covering every inch of his length.

"Go on." His grunt is released behind gritted teeth. "Come up to me with your tongue."

My mouth explores his calf, salt and his flesh form a party for my taste buds. To accompany my tongue, my fingertips dance up on the rest of his skin; my breasts and nipples graze Hudson's sinewy leg.

"Yes," he rasps when I suck on the inside of his thigh.

His ball sack smacks my forehead at each pulse of his hand on his cock. The intimacy of it, the eroticism of him jerking on me and having his balls land on my head time after time, it's unbearable. I twist my head, opening wide.

"Christ, your mouth was made for sucking my balls." He slows his strokes. "Hollow your cheeks, baby, take them all in."

I follow his demand, swiping my tongue forward to have it flat on his cock. His fingers curl inside my hair, pressing my scalp, pressing me to him in one final push, then releasing me.

Strong hands full of intent grab my shoulders, yanking me up.

"You really did wake up in a debased mood." He examines me, his face seeming sharper and edgier than when we faced each other earlier. "Want to use up every minute of being my whore before I treat you like my queen outside."

The acute pain in my nipples grows, the closer Hudson draws me to him. There's a field of electricity connecting us, but unless his chest touches mine, unless I get that friction, I won't be sated.

"I do," I spit through the mounting desire. "Please. Sir."

"Off to the shower." His lips hardly move. "Face to the wall."

My shoulders feel cold without his touch. With only one way to have it back, I turn from him, stalking into the shower hall.

Hot water greets me, pelting my head, soaking my hair. I don't stop to revel in its warmth, stepping forward to the wall. I close in on the shower tiles, about to touch them.

"Not like this." Hudson swipes my hair to the side. His teeth are at my throat, cock is between my butt cheeks. "Hands pressed forward."

He moves backward with me, kicking my legs open. He lays two of his fingers flat across my slit, gliding up and down, up and down.

And inside me.

"There's my filthy girl." One deep, up-to-the-knuckle stroke is what he gives me.

And just as fast, his fingers are gone. His hands slide to seize either side of my hips. He yanks me back while thrusting his hips forward, resuming the motion with so much grace and even more intention.

I'm rattled and turned on, grasping for air yet unable to fully breathe.

"More," I rasp, pleading to appease my swelling clit, my wanting tits.

Hudson pulls away, pressing the head of his cock to my asshole, and landing a slap on my butt. I heave out a loud breath, although I don't run. I press my ass to him, egging him on to enter me.

"Naughty, naughty." He spanks me again, water splashing at the swift contact.

He draws back and I stifle a scream of frustration. It builds up, about to escape until cold, smooth liquid lands on my lower back. Hudson's fingers resume their exploration of me, smearing the lube we keep in the shower down to my crack.

All teasing, all testing, and elegant probing are done and over with. He enters my behind, the whole length of his index finger, joined by his middle one right after.

"My whore likes it in the ass." The pressure on my butt intensifies from having Hudson lean his body on me.

His mouth is to my ear. He says in a raggedly tone, "Likes having me open you up in your tight pucker,"—he thrusts faster, slithering his other hand forward to flick my mound repeatedly—"so much that you don't even care if it's my tongue, my fingers, or my dick. Isn't that right?"

I roll my eyes to the back of my head, collapsing against this sensory assault.

"Yes," I moan like a wounded animal, consumed and feeble. "Can I—can I please come?"

"Go." Water drops land from his mouth to my skin. "Come now, and I'll give you my cock."

Fireworks upon fireworks light up behind my eyes. I'm shaking, melting, milking my husband's fingers. He carries me through this mind-blowing orgasm not by soothing me. Not Hudson.

Another batch of lube hits my now-empty crack.

"Relax," he commands.

I flip my hair, twisting my head to watch him standing proud, holding his cock in one hand, the second one traveling from my waist to the side of my ass. The stream pelts his body, cascading down his hair, rippling waterfalls across his chest and biceps.

"Lean forward and"—he emphasizes his next words by shoving me, stretching me open with his blunt crown as he pushes into me—"relax."

"Yes, Sir," I mumble to myself, obeying him.

Submission which he rewards me for. Inch by pulsing inch, he assumes complete control over me.

"Just like that." He pounds, grunts, and commands what's his. "Take all of it."

"Hudson," I yelp. The initial pain is gone. Now I'm crying out for him to save me, to allow me this other orgasm I'm begging for.

"No." His rumble is stronger than the water hitting us and the floor. "And I don't want to hear another *please*. You're my whore, and you'll only come when I"—thrust—"specifically"—pound—"say so."

Darkness fills my eyes. The intensity of what he's doing to me, of the great lengths I have to go through to comply with his demands, nearly blinds me. Yet I remain absolutely silent, piercing my bottom lip with my teeth to wake myself up.

"My obedient slut," he says. "You're doing so well."

A whimper slips past my lips. Hudson pins his chest to my back, slithering a hand around my neck. He smooths his palm over the front of it, not choking me, but applying just enough pressure so I know whom I belong to.

"Come with me."

I sigh, and it's full of relief and love when my orgasm hits me.

I'm not the least prepared for the ferocity I'm being slammed with. It's as if I'm smashing into a brick wall at three hundred miles per hour. My sigh transforms into a gag, then into a choked-out scream.

Light and love and a burning comet rush through me, illuminating my world brighter when Hudson grunts and shoots his load into my ass.

We stand there, him inside me, me feeling way too high for any sort of response other than to fall into Hudson. My Dom. My best friend. My husband.

CHAPTER NINE

Hudson

"You continue to amaze me, little." I soften inside her, slowly pulling out. My arms are wrapped around her middle, protecting her feeble body from falling. "Every day anew, you amaze me."

Her complete submission, her absolute devotion, and her dirty side make me want to worship at her feet day and night.

"Thank you." The words are pushed out of her like she has no strength left.

"My love."

Turning her in my arms, I examine her face. Her eyes glimmer beautifully, so alive. The orgasm may have shattered her body, but it hasn't fucked with her light. I brush her hair from her face, dropping wet kisses on her cheeks.

"Are you okay to stand on your own?"

Most of our aftercare sessions consist of Avery sitting or lying down, yet the thought of sending her out there to dry, then having her back here to wash herself properly in half an hour doesn't bode well with me.

"Yes." Her eyelashes shine as water droplets sprinkle on them.

Slowly and carefully, I release her, allowing her space. I outstretch my hand to the right, grabbing her shampoo.

"Turn around." I signal with my head, and she does.

The citrusy shampoo pours out of the pink bottle and into my palm. I put it back on the stainless steel holder, and begin lathering Avery's hair.

She opens her mouth in an expression of pure bliss, relaxing into me, relinquishing another kind of control to my hands. It isn't sexual; it isn't a response to do as I say. In these moments, she is simply *mine*.

As I am hers.

Once done, I rinse the suds out, murmuring *Good girl* in her ear while I do. The conditioner is next. I apply it only to the strands of her hair, then pin it up the way she likes it.

Following my care of her, I massage her body with soap. Avery tilts her head in the opposite direction of where my hands go as I massage her neck.

She rolls her arms when I rub into her tight muscles, lets out a short laugh when I go for the armpits, and another delighted moan when I slide my hands forward to apply the soap on her breasts, stomach, and navel.

But there's only so much I can do standing up. I round Avery's still body, my hand gently wrapped around her neck to support her.

Her somewhat drowsy eyes stare back at me, her skin mildly reddened by the heat of the shower. Steam billows in the expansive stall, giving my wife an even more angelic look than her normal, ethereal self.

Having a sub drop—the descent after an intense scene, the main reason for aftercare—is common. It's expected of the party that tolerated either violence, humiliation, or blind obedience to their Dominant's demands despite the hardships piled up, to end up bare of endorphins and vacant.

What I'm experiencing at this moment is a Dom drop. While less discussed, it still happens, for any number of reasons. For me, following a session of degradation with my Avery, it occurs every now and then. The urge to nurture her, to treat her like the delicate flower she is, it's overwhelming, a deeply-rooted necessity.

And I'm blessed beyond measure that she allows me to do it.

"I love you," I tell her because there's no way I can hold it in.

"I love you." Her lips move.

My mouth flutters across hers. A gentle caress before I get down on my knees. It gives me an inordinate sense of empowerment to show my devotion to my wife by treating her well, even if it means being quote-unquote *beneath* her.

In fact, the satisfaction I'm experiencing is so intense that I get semi-hard again. But I don't act on it, nor do I feel an orgasm building up inside me. It's an exhibition of love, of all-encompassing affection. Nothing more, nothing less.

Taking her in from my place on the floor, I say, "Grab my shoulders, little."

"M-hmm." She strokes my damp hair, then obeys.

I spurt a new batch of soap into my palm, placing the bottle aside. I'm at eye level with her sweet, swollen pussy, kissing it tenderly as I massage Avery's thighs in circular motions from the back to the front.

She hums, her fingers digging into my flesh, although she, much like I do, doesn't do anything but revel in the attention I dote on her.

I separate myself from her, pour soap from the bottle, and scrub her knees, calves, feet. I lift each foot to the water spray, wait for it to clear out the soap, and kiss the top of her foot, all five of her toes.

When I'm finished, I straighten to my full height, engulfing Avery in a hug and drawing her to me.

"Go dry off," I say to her hair. "I'll meet you outside soon."

"No." She shuffles to look at me, sneaks her palms between us, and pushes against my chest.

One of my eyebrows quirks up. "You want to watch me shower?"

"I want to do it myself." Her voice and fire slowly creep back.

A shred of contentment sneaks into my soul for helping her rebound from our scene peacefully through my devotion. The rest of me, the part that's recovered alongside Avery, it rebels.

"Please, I need this," she repeats the plea from earlier.

I'm not sure what her reasons are, not sure she knows them herself. But I don't doubt her.

"Okay, then."

Avery, whose arms are shorter than my own, walks to the holder instead of reaching out. She takes my shampoo, filling her delicate palm with it. The minty fragrance of my blends into Avery's citrusy hair products and they're no longer two separate ones—they're one.

Circling me, Avery raises her hands to apply the shampoo to my head. I tip my head back to help her, while she leans into me for support. I experience her love and adoration for me through the reverent paths her fingers trace along my scalp.

It's then that I realize this doesn't take away from my role as caretaker after we've had sex, but adds to her role of submissive. This is why she asked for it, and if she hasn't figured it out already—which I highly doubt, given my wife's intellect—it'll be another topic of conversation for us tonight.

Soap runs across my back muscles, my shoulders, my arms. Avery makes it a point to dig into where it's tight, caress a little longer where I huff from pleasure.

Her dainty feet splash on the wet floor as she returns to my front, my ears hear her come before my eyes see her determined expression. Soap-filled hands, she traces my pecs, my stomach, my legs on her descent.

She sends me a glance that can only be described as love from below, pressing her lips to my semi-hard cock. Avery keeps at it, mirroring my handling of her by lathering my legs with soap without stopping her gentle kisses on my shaft and crown.

"Baby," I grunt, eager to say something, anything in this heaven I'm living in, thanks to her.

She's quiet, soaping me diligently down to my toes, kissing them.

"All done." She stands up, an enchanting smile grazing her lips.

I grip her jaw, angling her head higher and slamming my mouth into hers. The kiss isn't long, but it's brimming with the whirlwind of emotions

I'm experiencing, ones that aren't nearly as simplified as love.

"Shower time might be done." I press my forehead to hers, ignoring the water dripping between us. "But you and me, little blue, never. I'll never be over you."

CHAPTER TEN
Avery

*H*udson dries me in a towel, presses his lips tenderly to my forehead, eyes, cheeks, and nose.

"We have around forty-five minutes until we have to leave." He rubs his towel on his wet upper body and ties it around his hips. "You're good with the time?"

"Yes." I hug the plush fabric to my body, tiptoeing toward the vanity. "Having you choose the dress and shoes and earrings kinda shortens the process in half."

On my twenty-fifth birthday, a week before Christmas, Hudson bought me one of the most stunning gowns ever to exist. True to form, he had the floor-length dress adjusted to my size and height, although, unlike the many other blue items he purchased for me, this one was golden.

When I asked him about it, he said the sequin embellishment all over the gown, the sandals, and the star-shaped earrings felt like the countless Christmases he wants us to have together.

My husband can seem cold and calculative, some may even deem him deadly serious at times, but deep within his heart, he's a romantic through and through.

As if summoned, he appears at my back just as I'm popping open the deodorant. His face is a mask of somberness only I am able to interpret as fake.

"Is that a complaint I hear?"

"No, Sir." I send him a wink through the mirror. "A compliment."

His lips twitch. "My pleasure."

Hudson snakes an arm around my middle, dragging me to him. I think for a moment that he's in the mood for another round, part my lips to tell him we don't have the time when he presses on the bottom drawer of the vanity beneath the sink.

It rolls toward us, and he removes my hairbrush from it.

I watch his hands separate a group of hair to my front. His green eyes are fixed on the mirror, skating between mine to the hair he's brushing, starting at the ends.

"If you're in a hurry, I can just do it myself."

"Like I mentioned,"—he captures my attention with his words and blaring glare alike—"it's my pleasure."

He undoes the knots in my thick, brown hair, using the brush to soothe my scalp. A profound sense of calm renders over me.

"There you go."

Tenderly, he pats my head, places the brush back, and goes for his deodorant. A dose of the fragrance that's connected to some of the best memories of my life wafts in the closed bathroom, filling me with love.

My eyes close on their own accord, my brain reveling in the scent of him.

I open them a brief moment later, and Hudson is gone.

I blow dry my wet hair, running my fingers through it for a touchup of extra volume. Then I spend a minute or five in front of the mirror, like my physical appearance would give me answers as to what the fuck is going on with me.

The constant craving for sleep doesn't leave me unless Hudson and his magical touch are there to wake me. Climbing the stairs has become a chore and the third cup of coffee I had today smelled as though… I don't know. I didn't pour milk in it, so there was nothing in it to cause it to smell differently.

Maybe it really is simply a matter of sleep. It sounds reasonable, that and the heightened sensitivity, and the on again off again dizzy spells.

Shaking my head, I hang the towel on the rack. I'll see whether Hudson's new work solution will prove a success over the next couple of weeks. Hopefully, it will, but just in case it doesn't, I'll set an appointment with my GP and ask for blood tests. Which I haven't done in… ever.

Hudson is already in his navy-blue suit pants and pulling on his undershirt when I enter the room. Quietly, I admire the sight of the breathtaking man who calls me a whore and a queen in one breath and makes me feel perfectly excited to be both.

And I love him.

"See anything you like?" He shrugs on his light gray dress shirt, buttoning up.

My husband acts all innocent, casual even. His extremely slow and sensuous once-over tells a different story.

"I can ask you the same question." I flip my hair, moving to the dress and thong he hung for me on the inside of one of the closet doors. Our commitment collar is already on.

Hudson's chuckle follows me, and I smile to myself.

See, nothing wrong with you. You don't have snide comebacks when you're sick.

That affirmation calms my nerves by a notch, enough to reassure the smile lingering on my lips, enough for me to get dressed and dolled up for our dinner.

"John Flaherty's assistant sent me an email earlier today, she wanted to know about—"

"Little one." Hudson's voice is a quiet warning from his place across the table. "Do you remember our agreement?"

"Yes, but—"

"No buts," he says in *the* voice while offering the waitress who places the meat courses in front of us a curt nod.

She, Regina, explained in length about each dish on the fixed menu up until this moment. This round, facing Hudson's stern expression, she announces the Wagyu ribeye she places in front of us, then scurries to the kitchen.

"Your health is above all else, Avery."

He shows no interest in the food served to him. Nor does he care for the view of the city, the pristine linen, or the low-hanging lights in the expensive restaurant he reserved for Valentine's.

He's oblivious to every thought-out detail in the magnificent place we're sitting at. Everything except me.

"*You* are above all else." He leans forward, linking my fingers with his in an unrelenting hold to match his fierce gaze and voice. "I told you before you're my entire heart, and I meant it to my bones."

My eyes glisten, and I blink furiously to stop my vision from blurring.

It works. Partially.

"I don't just *love* you." Hudson squeezes my hand, spitting the word like it offends him. "I breathe for you, I'm responsible for you. Your mental and physical health are mine to look after, mine to cherish and be on top of *always*. I don't take it lightly. Not now, not ever."

He pauses, making my tears, my heart, and the world stop with him.

"Not in this lifetime, little," he whispers, his intention burning through him. "Our business can shut down tomorrow and I wouldn't give a damn. If you so much as catch the flu and it has to do with our company and the stress suffocating you, I'll never be able to live with myself."

"Thank you, Sir."

His title slips shamelessly from my lips. I don't care who hears, I don't care what the rest of the diners in their designer gowns and expensive suits will think of me. I'm his and that's the unique and exquisite truth of my existence.

"My beautiful wife." Hudson draws my palm to him, pressing his lips to my knuckles.

He reclines back in his chair, while the electrifying current where he kissed me continues to tingle my skin.

"So, besides work." He still doesn't touch his ribeye. Neither do I. "What are you missing?"

"Nothing," is the first answer at the top of my head.

Hudson and I are doing well financially; we have a roof over our heads, clothes to dress us, and food to put in our mouths. Oh, and health insurance. Can't forget about that.

Other than the essentials, I belong to Hudson. And following that, even without all of the above, there'll be no happier soul than mine.

"I'm not talking about material things." A hint of a warm smile finally breaks through his solid fortitude. "I know you, which is why I knew no gift I would've bought for today would've been enough. I wanted to give you something significant. I just need you to tell me what it is."

I take a deep, thorough examination of my life. Of all the things I'm grateful for, all the things I have. And the one thing I don't. Yet.

"A baby. Or two," I say in a hushed voice.

The irony of the situation, of how I called him Sir with confidence yet I mention such an obvious, everyone-has-one kind of thing as though it's a dirty secret.

"Babies," Hudson repeats.

His impenetrable stare scares the living shit out of me. For once, I wish he'd be a transparent teddy bear of a guy instead of my Dominant husband. I wish on it really fucking hard.

He maintains his firm grip on his maddening silence, only opening his mouth when he turns, raises a hand to the waiter, and says, "Check, please. Now."

CHAPTER ELEVEN
Hudson

It doesn't come as a surprise to me to hear my wife wants to have kids. We discussed it in the past, about having a family. In broad strokes, as in, *someday in the future*, or *we're going off contraception, but we're aware it'll be a while before the pills clear from your body*.

An ambiguous concept we threw into our conversations.

It's a whole other thing to have Avery lay her claim on her need for kids.

Our kids.

And it, in turn, fuels my need to lay claim to *her*. I'm hot and hard to have her, and yet incapable of responding to her the way I'd like to here, in this restaurant.

"Hudson?" Her timid voice cuts through the five-minute silence as I sign the credit card receipt.

"Before you start thinking anything's wrong,"—my chair scratches the floor as I stand up, dropping the pen while I do—"there isn't."

I round the table, offering Avery my hand. She accepts, my delicate, sparkling woman rising on both of her feet. The sequins of her dress reflect the light in the restaurant, but their shine is dulled by the glimmer in my wife's eyes.

Blood rushes through my veins, my cock stiffening painfully. There's this blankness wrapped up in determination around my brain, and in this silent chaos, three words echo like a mantra.

I. Want. Her.

"You sure?"

"There is one thing bothering me, actually," I whisper. Civil on the outside, desperate for her from within.

"Oh?"

"Yes." A smirk tugs at my lips, knowing I'll turn her befuddlement into a monster of lust matching my own in a second. "That we're still here instead of starting to work on any number of babies you want back home."

Her jaw slacks. I shut down that beautiful mouth of hers by sealing another kiss on it, then escort her out of the restaurant.

The valet arrives with our Tesla, and I open the door for Avery, closing it softly behind her. I'm calm and calculated with each move.

But fuck if I don't have an urge to try our new toy on my wife while putting a baby inside her.

We drive in silence during the short distance from the restaurant to our home. Three blocks straight ahead left, then another four blocks straight.

I hardly pay attention to the road, sneaking glances at Avery, at the moonlight hitting her dress and coloring it in a silver hue. At her soft cheeks. At her curious blue eyes that she aims back at me.

I'm in love. I'm fucking in love.

I park in our driveway, walk around the hood of the car to Avery's side, and help her out. I go through the motions of entering through the front door, disarming the alarm, climbing the steps while my hand clutches possessively to Avery's.

She doesn't speak, causing a slither of worry to creep up my spine. I look down at her when we step onto the landing.

"Little."

A beaming face stares back at me.

"I'm good," she answers, guessing my question. "I thought that I scared you off." She bites her lip, wiping out whatever's left of her pale-pink lipstick. "Talking about kids. Right now."

"Never doubt how badly I want a family with you, Avery Kent." I run my thumb across her bottom lip, pulling the soft flesh out of her hold.

"Thank you." She goes for a kiss just as I'm turning to guide her into our mirror room.

I gesture for her to enter before me, and she teeters on her heels to the center of the room. I switch on the light over where Avery's standing. It casts an amber glow around her, like a halo, like the angel she is.

The rest of the lights I switch on too, though not as intense. Enough for us to see each other without ruining the mood.

My dick strains in my pants, from seeing her move her hands to the small of her back and open her legs for me, head bent low. One of the ready positions.

"Is this how you'd like me, Sir?"

Not that it matters, given we're the only two people who live here, but I close the door behind me. I move toward Avery, my steps purposefully louder, to build anticipation for her. To have her know I'm coming even though she doesn't see me.

"Close. Very close."

Instead of going to her directly, I walk over to our sex toys closet. I extract sanitizing wipes and the new black, leather collar I bought as a surprise for today. It's not meant to substitute the commitment one she has on.

A leather belt is attached to its back by a silver hoop, and another silver hoop is attached to the bottom of the belt. There, it connects to two other shorter leather belts that lead to two padded, leather handcuffs and a long leash.

"Before we start." Stopping in front of her, I tilt her head up using one finger. "I have a new toy for today, one we discussed, but I need your okay on it."

The toy she hasn't seen before isn't something I want to surprise or intimidate her with while both of our adrenaline runs high. I love fucking her senseless. I love her consent even more.

I distance myself from Avery so she can have a good look at it. "Is that acceptable?"

Wide, dark eyes threaten to consume me. "Yes, Sir."

"Your safeword, if you change your mind?"

"Whitlock."

"Good girl." I place it aside for later, sidestepping her willing form, and stop behind her. My fingers locate the top of the zipper at her back, tugging it down and stripping her of the dress.

I'm methodical. Functional. She needs to be naked. That is that.

She wears no bra, only a sheer lace white thong, embroidered in gold, partly covered by her crossed hands.

I spank her ass. Twice.

Her little cry makes me even harder.

"You asked if that's how I wanted you." Her round flesh begins to redden on the third slap. "I said it's close, and that's it? No follow-up questions?"

"I'm sorry."

"Apology accepted." I slip an arm around her stomach, pinning her to my chest. My cock molds into her backside, possessing her even with her thong and my pants between us. "Now, what would a good girl ask?"

"How would you like to have me, Sir?"

"First, on your hands and knees, little." I wind her hair in my fist, dragging her down to the floor. "I had plans for tonight—plans I'll execute after I have my semen deep inside you."

With my help, she gets down to her knees, placing her hands in front of her.

"Good girl." My hand releases her, and I unbuckle my belt, undo my pants and curl my fingers around my cock. "Look at me."

She does, raising her head from the floor to watch me from the reflection in the mirror.

"If I shove my dick in you, Avery." I jerk myself slow, then fast, taunting her lust-filled gaze. "How wet are you going to be?"

Her shuddered breath is more than an answer.

I bend to my knees behind her, grab a fistful of her hair again, and smack her ass while my shaft is pressed to her crack.

"What did we say about words?"

"I'm wet, Sir." The shadows obscuring our faces obscure parts of us, adding another layer of mystery to our game. "So wet for you."

Leaning forward, I move her thong to the side and press my thumb to her cunt. Her body flinches, releasing a choked vowel from her throat, and yet she remains in place.

"My good girl is trying hard, isn't she?" I drag my thumb lower, applying pressure and stretching her clit. "Dying to make me proud of her."

"Yes." She lets out a breath as if she's wanted to say yes to that her whole life.

Finding her dripping slit, I hook two fingers inside her. "Yes, you are. My soaking wife, needs my cum in her womb."

"Yes, please, Hudson." Her expression morphs in the mirror, pained and hungry all at once. "Fuck me. Put babies in me, please."

We both know that according to her cycle, there's no way whatever we do today will have any impact. We also discover what a turn-on it is to talk like this. I see it in her eyes, smell it in her arousal, feel her clenching, coating my fingers with more and more of her delectable juices.

"Oh, I plan to." In one crass gesture, I lean back and rip her flimsy thong off.

I straighten behind her, parting her butt cheeks, getting the full view of her spread cunt.

"You'll have every drop of my cum tonight. Every bit of it will be yours."

CHAPTER TWELVE
Avery

I scream in pleasure, my cry bumping against the mirror walls, the ceiling, the floors, and barrels back into my chest in a thundering whoosh.

Hudson's heavy dick infiltrates my pussy in one powerful, unforgiving thrust. He hits me hard, forcing himself into the sensitive spot where, one day, I'll be fortunate enough to bear his children.

"That's it." He draws back, his fingers sinking into my naked ass. Then he slams into me again. "You look so beautiful taking my cock, blue."

The rest of his thrusts into me are no longer slow or subtle. He fucks me from behind, balls slapping my pussy, his eyes penetrating mine. Hudson doesn't look at himself, has not an ounce of self-admiration. He cares for my reactions, for how I'm affected by this.

And I hold onto my Sir's gaze for all I'm worth.

"Christ, what a sight you make," he grunts, one vehement thrust after the other.

He spits on his thumb. Some of it sprays on my back, firing up a tingling sensation on my skin. Hudson's saliva and cum and sweat forever are a constant cause for my pussy to drip with need and my nipples to pebble into tiny, aching points.

"Once this is in your ass," he speaks while staring ahead, enunciating every word by rocking himself in and out of me. "You have my permission to come."

My insides are strung like a live wire, drinking in his declaration.

Thing is, he doesn't give it to me that easily. He grips my waist, leveraging my body and using it for his needs. My tits sway beneath me, my hair cascades down my face, sweat trickles down my forehead.

I have no choice left. I beg.

"Please," I ask even though he said it's okay. I love hearing every time anew.

His decadent smirk flashes in the darkness of the mirror room.

"Please,"—he fucks me so hard I'm being thrust forward a bit—"what?"

"Sir." My rasp is barely audible.

"One sentence, little."

I dig for the words, for the ability to compile a coherent sentence as he asks. To satisfy him.

"Please, Sir. Let me come."

He spits on his thumb that's dried up, sliding the thick finger into my ass. He's taken such good care of my ass when he fucked me in the shower that his thumb fucking me now doesn't hurt in the slightest.

I heave out a throaty sound I don't recognize, feeling absolutely full and immeasurably his. Moans and cries are my way of thanking Hudson as I come with his thumb drawing circles inside my ass and his cock emptying itself inside me.

He calls my name, caressing my back as he slowly leaves my body.

My holes feel empty without him in them, but the reflection of his adoring expression through the mirror more than makes up for it. He flips me gently on my back, then helps me to sit on my knees.

"Your orgasm face." His tongue swipes along his bottom lip, his large hand tucking a sweaty strand of hair behind my ear. "A fucking work of art, blue. Ready for part two?"

I'm practically boneless at this point, a little lightheaded even, which I contribute to the intensity Hudson devotes to each and every one of our scenes. I'm not afraid though, nor am I hesitant.

I do want more, and my husband will be there to catch and handle me until pleasure permeates through me again.

"Yes, Sir."

"Hold still."

He gets up, picks up a wipe from the floor to clean his thumb, and throws it aside. Afterward, he reaches behind me for the collar's buckle, removing the damp piece of lace and leather.

He eyes it for a long second, placing it on the floor. I want to know what he's thinking, but I don't want to ruin the moment. So, I wait.

Quietly, like the royal he is in my eyes, Hudson paces in an elegant stride to gather the other elaborate collar. Kneeling behind me, he moves my hair to my front, clearing my neck for him to wrap the new collar around it.

The leather belts and cuffs graze my naked and tender back, while Hudson's fingers warm my skin.

"Safeword?" he checks on me through our mirror, pausing his work on the contraptions about to be strapped to me.

"Whitlock."

The lock clicks at my back. In absolute silence, Hudson's deft fingers cuff my hands, arrange my arms, and stroke my back reverently. The whole process feels incredibly erotic in its intimacy.

Hudson's absolute focus on me, on the tightening of the buckles, of setting me to his will, it's intoxicating to watch and even more addicting to experience.

By the time he's done, my arousal and his cum trickle slowly out of my pussy to my inner thigh. My breasts are swollen and heavy, and I'm lightheaded with lust.

Hudson gets up to face me, the leash connected to the contraption in one hand. Looking at him, I get more excited to realize my desire for him is fully mutual. I breathe heavily, admiring his marvelous, veiny cock.

My husband steps closer, whipping his hot and silky member at my lips, keeping me alert and in the present.

"Mouth wide."

I open up, though apparently, it isn't enough. Hudson tugs at the leash connected to my collar, the pull reflecting his calculated intention; there's no damaging pain involved, no excessive choking or pressure on my spine.

There's caution and precision, and it gets me to where he wants me.

To gasp and part my lips so his shaft fits right in.

He glares at me, jaw tight, his god-like features are sharp and glacial. My Sir.

Between clenched teeth, he asks after taking his cock out, "You good?"

"Yes." Better than good.

By tasting him and myself on his cock before he took it from me, I floated in a galaxy of immense pleasure, traveling in time and space by Hudson's side. Not that I can articulate any of the flowery descriptions in the dazed state I'm in.

"Remember your safe signal?"

"Close my lips and suck hard."

"Good girl," he says, tugs, and forces my mouth to part.

He pounds into me, owning my soul, my breath, and my body entirely. The restraints behind me allow me to immerse myself fully into being Hudson's submissive. I'm at his mercy to maneuver the way he wants, to face-fuck how he likes, hitting the back of my throat repeatedly.

He lets go of some of the pressure from the leash. Hudson, who masters our rituals, pummels into my face ten times, draws back for air to seep into my lungs, and resumes his thrusts.

Still, tears of exertion run down my cheeks, and my saliva drips down my chin. And I love it. I live for it.

The heat in me rises to insane heights. His Dominance turns me on like the touch of my tits as they graze each other do, like the familiar taste of his precum landing on the tip of my tongue.

My orgasm bangs at the doors of my sanity, begging to be freed, to ransack my body. For Hudson, for my Sir, I hold on to it.

"Such. A. Good. Girl." Each word is emphasized by his cock slamming into me. "You make me proud, how you hold back from coming for me."

I hum at the pleasure of his praise, at the dizzying feeling that accompanies it.

"I'm going to reward you for it." There's a slight pressure at my neck as Hudson draws me from his pulsing member. "You want to come, baby?"

"Please," I mumble.

"Then you'll do it when I shoot my load in your face."

I almost faint, the eroticism of the demand consumes me so much.

"Close your eyes." He begins to jerk off, pointing the glistening head of his cock to my face.

My thighs finally have the permission to clench, to grind against each other. I don't require much else to send my body into the frenzy an impending orgasm brings with it. I'm balancing on a rope above the utmost enchanting fall.

"Gonna come, blue," Hudson grunts, saving me from the strict restriction, and I do.

I take the leap, I lose control, and I come.

CHAPTER THIRTEEN
Hudson

"How are you?" I dip the washcloth in the bowl of hot water, dabbing it on Avery's face.

"I'm good." Her lips twitch in her attempt to smile.

Watching my cum on her innocent face will forever feed into the possessive man in me. And although I take my time cleaning her on any other day, today I rush through it.

She deserves a good night's sleep and a day off tomorrow.

Hell, even a long weekend.

However long until she returns to herself. I'll fill in for her. I'm capable and wholeheartedly willing.

But I don't get to make these decisions on my own. I get to suggest them. Pointedly.

Once Avery's face is wiped clean, I put the bowl on the nightstand, joining her on our bed.

"Come here." I move her around gently so her head lies on my chest.

I rake my hand through her lush hair, down her shoulder, offering her a soft, safe place to land. Our bedroom smells of us, of sex and sweat, of love.

"Hudson?" she peeps from under me.

It's expected of her to be weak after the sex-filled day we had. I did ram my cock into her mouth without holding back while she committed to our scene with everything she had in her.

And yet the nagging concern in my heart, my gut, and throat, isn't satisfied by the explanation I give myself.

"Yes?" Her hair covers half her face, and I remove it.

I look at her, my jaw slacking at what I see.

In a matter of seconds, she turned pale. Really fucking pale.

"Avery?" Panic and the need to get her to open her eyes raise the volume of my voice.

"I don't think I…" she trails off. "I'm not feeling that great."

I've had it. Avery hardly ever complains. So this? Being unable to utter her plea for help?

"I'm taking you to the hospital."

I spring to the closet, throwing on sweats and a shirt. While considerations like getting her water and a bite of something sweet on the go plague my mind after we're out of this room, I snatch the first yoga pants and oversized shirt I find from her side of the closet.

Underwear is negligible at this point.

"N—no hospital," she murmurs.

I gallop the distance of the room in hurried steps, right back to where her fragile body lies.

"Yes, hospital." I wiggle the pants on her feet. "We'll see a doctor, they'll run their tests. You're going to be okay."

She has to be.

She doesn't answer, doesn't put up another fight, nor helps me put on her clothes.

"Avery?" I call her name again after her pants are up to her waist.

I stroke her cheek, but she's not responding.

A shout, lacking any self-restraint erupts. "Avery?"

She blinks when I slap her cheek. "Hudson?"

"It's going to be okay, baby," I repeat, straightening her back.

She's weak and feeble in my arms as I guide her arms up to slip her shirt on, but she speaks.

"I'm fine." The words are slurred. "Just…need…to sleep."

"You'll sleep once we know what's happening to you." I get up, scooping Avery into my protective embrace. Seeing her blink, almost fainting again, I swallow past the mounting alarm in my throat and use my Dom voice. "Until then, Avery Kent, you have to stay awake, do you hear me?"

We're down to the first floor. I grab the car keys and wallet from the console, leaving the house barefoot.

"You need to wait, blue." The pavement is cold and coarse beneath my bare feet. I feel nothing. "You can't faint again until we're in the hospital. You can't fall asleep."

"M'kay." Her mouth moves.

She's collapsed into the passenger's side, where I bend forward to snap the safety belt across her ragged body. I speed to the driver's side, slamming the door with enough force that the Tesla shakes.

What the car's GPS says will take seventeen minutes, I manage in a little over ten. I speed through the streets of San Francisco, testing the car's speed as I run one red light after the other.

Through these ten torturous minutes, I vacillate between demanding Avery to answer me and cooing to her like the helpless fucker I am that I won't let anything happen to her.

And nothing ever will. I don't care if she fainted twice. Whatever it is, whatever illness courses through her veins, I'll find a way to fix it.

I continue to curse myself, inwardly and without reverence. I replay what happened today as the Tesla tilts up with the street, then practically hops down to a steep decline. I tell myself I should've trusted my instincts, should've been more sensitive to the signs.

I should've ignored her ups throughout the day, should've forced her into the car the moment she showed signs of exhaustion.

I failed her.

"Here we are." The car swerves smoothly into the entrance of the emergency room.

Lights blare from the inside, an ambulance is parked at the side though there aren't any paramedics in sight.

Wordlessly, I jump out onto the pavement and run to the passenger's side. A young, blond doctor in dark blue scrubs emerges from the wide, glass sliding doors just as I hoist Avery out from her seat, and I yell to him.

"Help! Please!"

He rushes to me, looking at Avery who fainted again in the second I wasn't watching. Her head hangs back, long, brown locks draping on my arms.

"My wife," I cut in before he could ask anything. "She keeps fainting. Or falling asleep, or both."

"We'll get her treated. Follow me inside." He throws his unlit cigarette to the floor, guiding me into the hospital.

The doctor who ushered us in rattles instructions to the nurse at the front, and in a matter of seconds a male nurse appears rolling a gurney for Avery.

"What's her name?"

"Avery Kent," she murmurs, semi-conscious again.

"Shh. I have this." I caress her hair during our walk, hating that the nurse pushes her and not letting me do it. "I have you."

Knowing everything will move along faster if I let the staff of the hospital do their job is the only thing overriding my sense of responsibility for her.

"She's twenty-five," I fill in the information and give him her health insurance card with the antiseptic hospital smell infiltrating my nose.

Quickly, I employ the inner Dom in me, the man who's in control regardless of the situation. Avery needs me to be that person now, and I do it for her. I tell the doctor about her nonexistent medical history, her healthy parents, her healthy diet, and her exercise in the form of bike rides.

Avery hums and nods slightly in the interim, slanting her gaze at me.

Then I get to the painful part. "She dozed off this morning and has been tired throughout the day, but we thought she was overworked."

"We'll have to run tests and start her on saline IV." The doctor seems calm, even in his haste to guide us through the corridors.

My focus remains solely on my wife's face, making sure her eyes aren't closing on me. "Just…help her."

"We'll do our best, Mr. Kent." He casts a meaningful stare my way. "She's in good hands."

I notice how he doesn't promise me anything. I partly appreciate it, partly want to smash my head into the wall for the frustration it barrels down on me. But I settle for a, "Thank you. Doctor…?"

"Rogers. Come on, we'll talk after we stabilize her."

We turn into a narrow hallway and into an empty room, where the nurse and I help pile Avery into the bed. She doesn't say a word, her blue eyes open and locked on mine.

The fluorescent lights overhead accentuate how pale Avery is, the color she lost. In the span of twenty minutes, the red hue in her cheeks has dissolved, and I begin to question whether it really was there while we had sex or if I was so consumed by our game and her eagerness to have imagined it.

"I love you, Avery." I squeeze her hand.

I'm not a crying man. Some days, especially before Avery entwined herself into my life, no one would've called me 'emotional'.

Today, though, it requires my entire inner strength to choke the tears threatening to leave.

To keep myself from breaking down, I focus on what's being done for Avery. I don't take my eyes off the nurses who stroll in and out of the room. How they take her blood, test for fever, insert the IV and connect her to the machines that beep at a steady pace.

Rogers lingers next to me while they do, asking a million questions. Have we traveled to any exotic locations lately, eaten at a new restaurant, whether Avery is pregnant or not.

To all of those, I answer with a firm no. The last one though, my reply is not that I know of, I don't think so.

"All right." His gray gaze dances from Avery to me. "Soon we'll have the initial results to know what we're dealing with. Until then try to rest, both of you."

"Thank you."

The door shuts behind him, making no sound other than a soft, nondisruptive whoosh. I bow my head to the floor, gathering myself. I refuse to scare her with my weakness, refuse to overwhelm her with any emotion other than complete and utter confidence.

She deserves nothing but the best version of me.

"Hudson?"

"Yes?" Despite my attempts to look self-composed, my expression is, in all probability, raw and exposed to her.

"I love your rough side, but you're kinda squishing my hand." A chuckle seals Avery's sentence.

Every other sound throughout my almost thirty-eight years on this planet is a nail scratching on a board in comparison to the bells in her weak laughter.

I loosen my grip on her in an instant. My free hand roams gently across her face, ensuring by touch that she's well. Her hot breath, less shallow than ten minutes ago, flutters on my palm, soothing me that Avery's here.

She doesn't ask me to remove it, and I marvel some more at the life emanating from her.

The panic's death grip on my heart simmers as the clock ticks, the longer I feel her soft inhales and exhales land against my skin. I dip my hand to the side, cupping her jaw, smoothing my thumb over my wife's cheek.

Color reemerges on her lips, her cheeks returning their natural ruddiness little by little thanks to the IV.

"You chased away the darkness," she whispers in a croaked voice.

"That's because you chased mine long ago, blue." Bending to her, I brush my lips on hers, careful not to lean an ounce of my weight on her. "You brought me back to life long after I thought I was doomed to not feel anything. And you still will a hundred years from now. You just wait."

CHAPTER FOURTEEN

Avery

"I love you," I say.

"I love you, too. And I'm sorry." Hudson kisses me in a painful tenderness. "I'm so goddamn sorry."

"Sorry?" My eyes widen, tilting up to meet his gaze. He's too close and even this simple task is an effort, but I have to look at him. "What for?"

An unfathomable melancholy pools on his tortured face. So filled with regret. So unlike Hudson.

"For this. For not taking you to see a doctor earlier today."

His large palms cup both my cheeks, his face eliminating the harsh light above me. Hudson's presence, as a whole, eliminates the noise of the machines, the hospital's smell. It saves me. And I won't let him go another second thinking anything other than that.

"Hudson." It's my moment to use *the* voice.

The IV drips slowly, carrying me back into clarity. With each passing minute, I climb back to stand on solid ground. To find my resolve.

"You saved me." I raise my palm to his stubbled cheek, clenching my fingers to it. "You dragged me out of the bottomless well I kept flailing into tonight. You held me steady and secure in the minutes I was conscious. You have nothing, absolutely nothing to be sorry for. Whatever it is I have…"

I place a finger on his lips to stop him from interrupting me. I know my husband. He wants to tell me to not even go there. That there's nothing wrong, or reassure me he'll fix it.

I don't need it.

I need *him* to be okay.

"Whatever it is, it wouldn't have mattered whether you took me to the hospital this morning or now. I just fainted, and even then, it was temporary." I suck in a shaky breath. "We're here now. You saved me. You're still my Sir, my Master, my hero. Always will be."

"I'll make up for failing you," he continues like I haven't said a thing. "Make up for it for the rest of our lives."

"You'll love me all right." I claw at his shirt, letting what's left of my strength speak for me. "But not out of pity."

"Never."

"I do have one request."

"Anything."

Being mindful of the IV, I scoot over to the side. "Climb in next to me?"

He assesses the state of the tube and stickers connecting me to the heart monitor, scans the length of my body beneath the hospital sheets.

"No." Hudson's brow furrows, decisiveness marring his tone. "I won't risk it."

His lips press into a thin line. The dominance he exudes almost clouds the fact that his hair is a mess and his clothes are borderline pajamas. If I couldn't see him with my own eyes, I'd think he's wearing a suit, his hair styled perfectly at our home office and he's about to demand I crawl to him.

"I can move the tubes around." I start pinning them closer to me. It stings where the IV needle is taped to my body, a pain I pretend isn't there. "See, there's plenty of space for you."

"Please, stop. There's more to it than space." He's not having it. His palm covers mine, halting my fussing on the hospital bed. "I'm not going to lie here idle. I won't be waiting. I need them to figure out what happened to you and I need to have the results the second the lab sends them so they get to work on a solution, ASAP."

His willful devotion has my body disintegrating into tiny particles of love. For a moment, they fly around us, shining fireflies. My smile must be the silliest I've ever worn.

But still, it doesn't stop the void from opening inside me, the one being alone in this cold bed causes.

"Why are you doing this, Hudson?"

"For you." He kisses the back of my hand, inhaling my scent. "I won't rest until you're better."

"You know what will make me better?" I clench my fingers to his, the hardest my saline powers allow me. "To have your warmth on me. To have you lend me your strength, to be less alone."

"Little one."

His torn expression is the crack I've been searching for.

"Please, get in." I flutter my eyelashes at him. "Sir."

His barely-there smirk is suppressed. "Yes, ma'am."

He slips up, his large frame taking almost the entire bed. Which doesn't matter. With the utmost care, he arranges me so I'm cradled to his side, my heart pounding to the rhythm Hudson's dictates.

"Thank you." I breathe a sigh of relief, reveling in the comfort my husband's presence offers me. "Hudson?"

"Yes, baby?" His palm strokes my hair repeatedly.

I munch on the inside of my cheek. "Don't tell my parents until we have answers, okay?"

"You sure about that?"

"Very." I snuggle closer to him, sealing us together as one. "It'll make them worry and it could really be nothing."

"But then we're calling them." His Sir voice returns. "This isn't an open discussion."

"Then we're calling them." My ear is at his taut chest, his lips on my hair.

After that, he tells me I'm his good girl. How he loves me. How there's no him without me.

And to these words of devotion, to these promises of our never-breaking bond, I fall asleep.

"Mr. and Mrs. Kent?"

"Yes?" Hudson whispers so as to not wake me up.

It's too late. The man's voice already roused me from my dreamless sleep.

"I'm up." I blink away the cobwebs, shifting to sit straight in the dimly lit room. "Any news?"

"Easy, now." Hudson's hug forces me to remain in a lying position, glued to him.

"We have some of Mrs. Kent's results back."

Each muscle in Hudson's body tenses. He fastens me deeper into his side in his attempt to protect me against the weight of what's to come.

"Some?" Knowing Hudson, he's holding back for my sake, his tone only a little over a growl. "What about the rest? What are we going to do with *some*?"

I sneak a peek at the doctor, the half-inch Hudson's defensive embrace permits me.

He's grinning. "I don't believe the rest will be required, see, Mrs. Kent isn't ill. She's pregnant."

"What?" Hudson and I whisper in tandem.

"Yes. We suspect Mrs. Kent's short fainting spells were a consequence of dehydration and exhaustion that might have, combined with the pregnancy, ended with a drop in her blood pressure." The doctor, who's been unfazed by Hudson's silent rage, approaches our bed. He flips his plastic board for us to see, plastering a finger to the hCG test. "This here indicates you're about four weeks along into your pregnancy."

"Four weeks?" I mumble while Hudson snatches the clipboard from the doctor's hand. "I had my period four weeks ago."

"Exactly." Dr. Rogers fills in for Hudson's silence. "That's around the time you start counting."

Hudson hands the doctor the tests back, sliding off the bed. His eyes wander over me, his hands touch their path.

He seems…horrified.

It can't be the pregnancy itself. He literally just told me he wants it.

Unless...

"Are you sure he or she is alive?" Hudson spins to face the doctor, shoulders back, his composure strong. "Our sex life leans toward the rough side. All consensual, but this is how our lifestyle goes. Is it possible I hurt it? Is that why she fainted?"

While the good doctor's smile doesn't waver, I'm beyond mortified, pushing myself onto the harsh mattress, praying to be swallowed whole. Worried, yes, but painfully mortified.

Rogers, the professional he is, pretends my face isn't resembling the shade of a tomato, sidestepping Hudson to stand by the edge of the bed on the other side.

"You aren't bleeding," he addresses me. My humiliation alleviates a bit at how he's talking to me and with Hudson over my head. "Have you had or suffered any cramps in the lower belly over the last twenty-four hours?"

I glance at him, then at Hudson. His green eyes plead with me to tell the truth.

And I do.

"No." I rub my stomach, praying for the life inside it, however small it is, is unharmed. "Nothing."

"I'd like to check your stomach, see if it's hard or soft." Dr. Rogers presses the top of the hand sanitizer, rubs his palms, and lets them hover over me. "May I?"

"Yes," Hudson and I answer unanimously.

Hudson grips my hand tight, kissing the back of it.

"All right." Rogers nods, lifting the blankets off me and starting his examination. "Your stomach is soft, which is a good sign. Does any of what I'm doing hurt?"

"No." I stare up at Hudson, tears welling behind my eyes, rolling off my cheeks unbidden. There's still a chance.

"Blue." My nickname flows from Hudson's lips. He catches the river of salty water with his thumb, wiping them while his reassuring Dominant look pierces me. "It'll be okay. I swear it will."

"So far it seems it might be the case." We both revert our attention to Dr. Rogers. "I'll send in the on-call gynecologist to run an transvaginal ultrasound, even though at this stage there isn't much to see. She'll explain the rest. In any case, I would like to keep you here for observation overnight. Then we'll decide how to proceed."

"When's the soonest she can get here?" Hudson swipes his phone from the over-bed table. "If it's a matter of hours, we'll call Avery's doctor."

"There's no need. Dr. Duval lives close by, she'll be here within the hour."

"Can you—"

"Hudson, please." I tug at his hand, disregarding my worry, elation, and uncertainty so they wouldn't permeate into my voice. "We can wait an hour. It won't matter, either way."

There's a comical aspect to our situation, to how our roles flipped and I'm acting as the soothing partner. And yet, I don't laugh. I admire my husband a million times more for the level of inner strength he holds, to assume this difficult, costly role every day anew.

"You're right." His eyes close, then open. "Thank you, Dr. Rogers."

"I'll be seeing you two soon," he says, leaving the room.

The minute he's gone, I crumble. Disintegrating into a mess of tears and hysterical sobs, I free the tap holding my feelings down, and boy, do they pour out.

"Little." Hudson scooches next to me, cradling me in his arms. His warmth envelops me again, absorbing my emotional whirlwind, accepting my waves as they come. "I got you, blue. You're okay. We'll be fine."

"A—a—and the baby?" Snot chokes my voice, but I don't care.

Neither does Hudson.

"Regardless of tonight's outcome,"—he kisses my nose, my damp cheeks—"we'll handle it together. We will be parents, Avery. There's no question about it."

"Parents." The word and Hudson's reassurance are a balm to my high-string nerves. "We'll be parents."

Hudson smiles, melting what little concern and panic might have been left.

"We will be, my love. We will."

CHAPTER FIFTEEN
Hudson

Avery's asleep by the time Dr. Duval enters the room. I can tell it's her by the ultrasound machine she and the male nurse drag inside, both walking to the hospital bed Avery and I are mashed into.

"Hello," she whispers, introducing herself. "Dr. Rosalee Duval."

If Dr. Roger's call interrupted Dr. Duval's sleep, she doesn't show it. Her black hair is tied up in a neat ponytail, her face looks fresh and her black eyes gleam, even in the dark of the room.

"Hey, Hudson Kent, Avery's husband." I hold up a finger. "One second."

Slowly and silently, I slide out of the bed. Avery murmurs something in her sleep, then relaxes on her back. I still can't get over how tiny she is under the covers, and how my heart crumbles at the sight.

Depending on what answer the ultrasound will give us tonight, I'll have to buck up more than I ever have before. I have to face the reality that there's a chance he or she or they might be lost, and be there for my wife nonetheless.

Even though I'll be the reason we lost our first chance at being Mom and Dad.

Before guilt tears my soul in half, I remember who I am to myself, and who I am for Avery.

And I grow the fuck up.

I straighten to my full height, shaking the short woman's hand.

"Sorry your wife isn't feeling well." Her courteous smile is sincere. "I'm here to have a look at her and hopefully this is only a small bump in a long, blissful road."

The positivity overflowing from her helps me breathe again. Duval has this aura of being professional, kind, and adamant wrapped up in one woman, and I'm grateful she's the one on-call tonight.

I allow her to be the reassuring, taking-care-of-business person in the room, to be the one helping my wife. I'm not ashamed or feel any less by it. I'm proud to step aside and be ruled by smart decision-making rather than my ego.

Like I told Avery many years ago, during the years we worked together at Whitlock, when I was trying to convince her that her input as a marketing associate mattered to me, the Chief Financial Officer—*One should never reject a source of sound advice*.

"Thank you," I still whisper, although I know we won't be able to do it for much longer.

"We're going to need to have her awake for this, Mr. Kent."

"Of course." My eyes pinch shut, and I rub them with my finger and thumb. "Sorry."

"No worries." She and the nurse, Abraham, continue shining their polite smiles at me, probably holding onto them as I turn to my wife.

"Avery, honey." Running my fingers along her temple and jaw, I resume calling her, "Wake up, blue."

"Hmm?" Her eyelids are heavy, preventing her from opening her eyes fully. "Hudson?"

"Yes." The impulse to protect and shield her pummels through me, potent and running fiercely through my blood. "We're at the hospital, remember?"

"Now, I do." Avery squirms, trying to sit up straight. "Is the gynecologist here?"

"She is." I grab her shoulder gently, helping her up.

"Nice to meet you, Mrs. Kent." Duval outstretches her hand to my wife while Abraham adjusts the mobile station. "I'm Dr. Rosalee Duval. How are you feeling?"

"Better. Sleepy, but better."

"Both are good signs."

Duval notices my glare, at my disapproval of the hope she gives us. Hope that might be crushed in a few minutes.

"Though we remain cautiously optimistic," she adds on to her previous statement. "Dr. Rogers filled me in that he'd informed you we might not see anything. We might also see a tiny dot called the gestational sac, or worst case, see blood inside the womb."

Avery gasps. I clutch her hand tighter.

"However, let's not get ahead of ourselves before we see what's inside." She hits the hospital bed twice to conclude, offering me a blue hospital robe. "Help her get into this, Mr. Kent, and we'll start our examination."

Abraham takes the cue to leave. Dr. Duval shuts the curtain around the bed, staying outside the closed perimeter.

"I'm scared," Avery whispers as I remove her pants.

"Don't be." I kiss her thighs, knees, shins, toes on my path. "We're together in this. We're invincible." With no panties on, all I have left is help her shimmy her into her robe.

I cup her cheeks once we're done, pressing my forehead to hers. "I swear on my life, Avery Kent, you'll never have to carry any burden alone. You'll never suffer by yourself. You're *mine* and I will look out for you, hold your hand, and be your defender until my lungs give out and my bones are buried in the ground. Not a second before that."

"I love you." Her dainty fingers latch onto the top of my palms. "I love you so much."

"I love you." I brush my lips to her nose. "You ready?"

"Yes."

I kiss her ardently, whispering, "Good girl."

Her lips quirk up and it hurts my soul to detach myself from her.

In the following hair-pulling minutes, Dr. Duval instructs Avery on how to position her feet, to scoot closer to the end of the bed. To relax. Then she begins her exam, looking at the monitor.

Avery and I hold our breaths, staring at the monitor with her. Silence permeates the room.

"Looking good so far."

"Really?" Avery pipes.

"Thank fuck," I curse under my breath.

"Yes, here." Dr. Duval continues to explain the minuscule black spot on the monitor, its size, and how it matches the menstruation date and hormonal tests.

All I'm capable of thinking about is that Avery's okay, that there's no damage, no need for surgery or medical intervention. When those thoughts slowly simmer out, the happier ones take over, of a new life, of a baby Avery and I created.

Meeting Avery was the most exhilarating day of my life, hands down. The thrill, the knowledge she was unlike any other. She spurred a new joy in me I hadn't experienced in years, and going to the office had been something I'd looked forward to for the three years we worked together.

Having her for the first time in her apartment—I honestly didn't believe life could get any better after that.

Dating her, being engaged to her, and marrying her—these were all the best moments I've been too goddamn fortunate to experience. They were what I pictured for myself when I still believed in fairy tales as a kid, what I feared would never come.

This peace and love and perfect compatibility; I've been complete, thanks to her.

I never in a million years would have imagined, though, that the sum of them wouldn't match up to this. To actually have a *family* with her.

"I'll give you a disc and photos of the ultrasound for your OB-GYN," Dr. Duval concludes.

"Is there a chance you have a private clinic?" Avery asks.

"Yes, I do, but wouldn't you rather continue with your doctor?"

Avery turns her blue gleaming eyes to me. "I like her. I like her a lot. She's the one who found our baby, Hudson."

"What my wife wants, my wife gets." I address the doctor, "Do you have a card? Or the number of your office?"

"Of course, here it is." She offers us the number, tells us she'll update Dr. Rogers on the findings, and leaves.

The love of my life and the future mother of our baby tightens her grip on my hand. "We're going to be parents. We're actually going to be parents."

"Yes." I kiss her over and over. "Yes, little, we are."

EPILOGUE
Hudson

Eight months later.

"Are you sure about this?" Dr. Duval—who's become Rosalee like we became Avery and Hudson to her—glances at the two of us in the office of her private practice.

We sit in her office downtown. Our last checkup on our baby girl is done. Our new office has been renovated and the baby room is painted in a delicate cream, decorated in white and gray tones.

The one thing missing is baby Rosalee to appear. Any day now.

"Yes." Avery, in her blue maternity dress snug around her curves, made rounder and more sensual by her pregnancy. "Thanks to you, this pregnancy, from beginning to end, has been absolute bliss. We thought about it long and hard, and we would be honored to name her after you."

Rosalee, the doctor that is, sniffs. Her cool, confident and gracious demeanor is cracked by the tribute Avery and I pay her. Her sniffle starts a chain reaction of my wife sniffling, and me sitting there smiling, albeit a bit awkward.

Although, it's okay. Eight months of this has done well to prepare me for this moment.

This one.

Not...this.

"Ow!"

"Avery?" My torso whips to the side, my eyes turning into saucers at her pained expression, at her hand clutching the top of her swollen belly.

"It's the Braxton Hicks contractions." Her gaze is locked on her stomach. On our baby. "Right? That's what it's supposed to be. I'm not—I don't think I'm ready."

"I'm coming." Rosalee's chair rolls back. In an instant, she's on us.

But it's that millisecond that passes between her standing up to her and rounding her desk to our side that *it* happens.

The edge of Avery's chair has thick water dripping from it, landing in heavy flops on the tile floor of Dr. Duval's office.

"She's coming, too, it seems like," Rosalee says, crouching at my wife's side.

Avery's face is tormented, each breath is a struggle. We've been to dozens of Lamaze classes, practiced breathing, and read our share of what to expect come due day.

Except in a situation like this, nothing can prepare you for what's coming.

Nothing except inner silence and tapping into your peaceful, caring, Dominant space.

"I got you, and you got this." I set my palm on top of hers, cupping her jaw with the other. "You're good to walk?"

"Yes." My hand and the doctor's are on either side of Avery when she leans forward in pain. "I think."

The three of us waddle to the new SUV we bought for our expanding family. I instruct Rosalee on where we keep the towels while allowing Avery to sink into me, then we spread them on the passenger's seat and I jog to the front.

"I'm calling the hospital to let them know you're on your way!"

I register Dr. Duval's words, though they play little importance in whether I'd have gone there or not. Our baby is coming and they're going to see us and take care of my family. Now.

On the ride over I don't stop telling her what a good girl she is, how proud I am of her bravery and strength. Of course, Avery wouldn't be Avery without her share of I can'ts, but when I squeeze her hand and the contractions aren't assaulting her nervous system, she thanks me, tells me it's okay.

We keep our back and forth as we enter the hospital, then roll into the delivery room. Rosalee arrives five minutes after we're settled, and after hours of screams, sweat, and encouragement, Rosalee Kent emerges into the world.

"Welcome, little one." I stroke her feathery light brown hair tenderly as she lies on her mother's breast.

She and my wife are, without a doubt, the purest of diamonds ever conjured on this planet. Rare, magnificent.

Unbreakable.

I'd like to see someone try. They'll have to go through me first.

"Our baby," Avery coos, her feeble palm brushing over mine. We both caress our newborn child together, the three of us connected.

One unit, from now until the end of our days.

"You make me the happiest, proudest man, blue."

"I love you, Daddy," she whispers.

"I love you."

About the Author
Writing edgy spicy novellas, addicted to HEAs, and an avid plant lady.

Stay in Touch!
Newsletter for new releases:
https://bit.ly/3c3K2nt
Instagram: https://bit.ly/3QQ3Nh4
TikTok:
https://www.tiktok.com/@evamarkswrites
Facebook Group: https://bit.ly/3LnFpln
Website: https://www.evamarkswrites.com

Have you read the Blue series?

Little Blue, Book 1

I worked for Hudson Kent for years.
He's not a man you refuse.
But I did.
Because no matter how much I wanted him, chasing the sexy, older CFO would've ruined the reputation I worked so hard to build. It just wasn't a risk I was willing to take.
Until now.
Hudson isn't my boss anymore. There's nothing stopping us from acting on our mutual attraction and acting out every dirty fantasy we've ever had.
So, if he calls me now, there's only one reply I can give.
Yes, Sir.

TW: Bondage, BDSM, a bit of degradation.

Available on Amazon

Have you read the Blue series?

Little Halloween, Book 2

This holiday he plans on a special trick and treat for her…

After overcoming our differences, I'm finally engaged to Hudson, my old boss and millionaire CFO.

We're madly in love and I can't complain when he constantly cherishes, coddles me and says I'm his good girl. I can't and won't, even if I miss his harsh domineering side at times.

But my fiancé, who reads me like a book, can tell I have doubts, and he knows just how to put them to rest.

This Halloween, at an adult club party, Hudson will show me and everyone around once and for all exactly what my Sir is made of.

TW: Bondage, BDSM, pet play, sex club, exhibitionism, a bit of degradation and a whole lot of love.

Available on Amazon

More Books from Eva Marks

Blue Series
Little Beginning, book #0.5 — Coming Soon
Little Blue, book #1
Little Halloween, book #2
Little Valentine, book #3

Adult Games Series
Toy Shop, book #1
A New Year's Toy, book #2

Standalones
Primal — Coming Soon

Made in the USA
Middletown, DE
15 February 2023